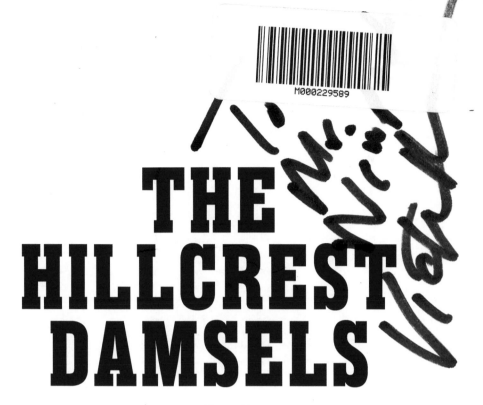

THE HILLCREST DAMSELS

A Trevor Stillwell Mystery

VICTOR BARROS, JR.

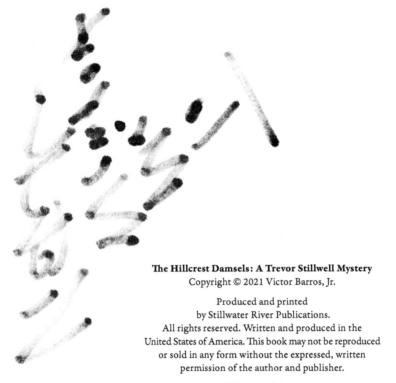

The Hillcrest Damsels: A Trevor Stillwell Mystery
Copyright © 2021 Victor Barros, Jr.

Visit our website at
www.StillwaterPress.com
for more information.

First Stillwater River Publications Edition

ISBN: 978-1-955123-04-4

1 2 3 4 5 6 7 8 9 10
Written by Victor Barros, Jr.
Published by Stillwater River Publications,
Pawtucket, RI, USA.

I dedicate my first novella to my friend Sherry and my cousin Catherine—two women who were instrumental in The Hillcrest Damsels *coming to life.*

Catherine encouraged me to share my work with the world. Her validation and support were invaluable.

Sherry was my inspiration and provided valuable technical assistance.

May God bless both of you and thank you from the bottom of my heart.

A special dedication to my hero, my mentor, and my cousin, Victor A. Prout, a.k.a. Ug-Vic. Rest in peace. You will always be in my heart and in my mind. Love you Vic.

I would also like to acknowledge the following individuals for their support:

J. Darrel Barros	*Edith Murad*
Rachel Russell	*Victor Barros, Jr.*
Michelle Fontes	*Zehua Barros*
Quintin Prout	*Bryan K. Barros*

H E WOULD OFTEN stare out the window, peering through the dust-layered venetian blinds which hung loosely from the attic windows of his childhood bedroom. A twelve-year-old boy lost in a repetitive daydream. The same vivid and detailed daydream he revisited again and again. He knew it as: The Apartment Daydream.

The attic space that functioned as he and his younger brother's makeshift bedroom was a decent size from a square footage perspective. It ran the entire length of the house, but much of that space was unusable due the pitch of the roof. The attic room was also lacking in natural sunlight because it had only two small westward facing windows that begrudgingly allowed only a hint of light, even on the sunniest of days.

With slanted ceilings on both sides, the space was designed more for storage than living. He often felt cramped and confined, and slightly claustrophobic. His brother's disheveled and disorganized behavior only served to exacerbate the sense that the bedroom walls were closing in on him. His brother's propensity for sloppiness and seeming inability to pick up after himself proved to be a constant source of irritation for him during his childhood. He loved his brother very much, but never had two brothers been more different. Their only commonalities were their love of comic books, horror/sci-fi movies, and restaurants.

VICTOR BARROS, JR.

It was this frustrating reality that first gave birth to The Apartment Daydream. To him the daydream was not a flight of fantasy or anything overly extravagant or lavish; in fact, the daydream was quite simplistic and, he thought, very achievable. The apartment of his daydream stood in stark contrast to the attic bedroom of childhood. It was bright and spacious, and definitely would not include his younger brother.

Instead, it had to include a large bedroom with ample space to comfortably fit a king-size bed with a sturdy firm mattress. Unlike his fifteen-year-old twin bedframe and mattress in the attic whose springs and coils had seen better days. It had long ago stopped providing any type of body support and squeaked and clanged anytime he shifted position, and when not making noise the bed rested pitifully in the corner of that attic bedroom, like an old hound dog who could no longer hunt.

This king-size bed of his daydream would have ample sets of sheets and a plush comforter adorned with colorful pillow shams and a matching duvet. He was eleven years old when these daydreams first started. He wasn't exactly certain what a duvet was. He had overheard his mother talking about it in relation to a comforter set she wanted to buy for her bedroom, so he just adopted the word as part of his own lexicon. It wasn't until some years later that he figured out what it was.

Also, within this imaginary bedroom was a sturdy cherry oak dresser and bureau set with ample drawers to store his clothes. The reality of his childhood situation was a hand-me-down dresser whose drawers would stick so much that he would have to grasp the handles and tug several times to get them to open fully. He had a number of black milk crates stacked against the wall which he used to store his sweaters. He was meticulous about his sweaters. They were all neatly ironed, folded and carefully organized in the crates, one placed on top of another. Each crate held four individual sweaters and he had three crates full of sweaters of multiple colors and different styles. The sweater crates, as with all his personal items, were completely off limits to his younger brother who had no appreciation for the time and effort he put into arranging and organizing his sweaters.

As much as he enjoyed having nice clothes, he loved nothing more than his comic book collection, one of the few things he and his brother could share and talk about. They both loved the Marvel Comics universe and the fantasy world of superheroes and villains that Stan Lee and Jack Kirby created in the early 1960s. Being the older brother by three years, he had more comics and the better overall comic book collection, a point that he would remind his brother of often.

While his younger brother would occasionally trace the cover and cut out sections of his comics, Trevor would store them in old hat boxes under his bed. During most of his childhood, comic books were only twenty or twenty-five cents apiece, so between his allowance and the money he earned from his paper route, each week he had enough money go on his favorite neighborhood trek. First he'd hit the local burger joint, Kelly's Hamburgers, for a Topper with cheese, fries, and a vanilla shake, then make a quick visit to the local penny candy stands located within the Five n Dime. The stand was better known to the kids in the neighborhood as P for P. After stocking up on candy shoelaces, Mary Janes, root beer barrels and Bit-O-Honey, the last stop was Iron Horse Comics, the shop where he would buy a few of the new releases. Once he completed this joyous junket, he would race home in hopes of arriving there before his brother so that he could enjoy his spoils alone and uninterrupted.

Although his family was considered lower working class, as a child K. Trevor Stillwell had everything he wanted. From his perspective, his childhood was as good as it gets and that was solely due his mother's love and attentiveness.

His father, Jessie Stillwell, had dropped out of school in

the sixth grade to help out his mother, who was struggling to provide for their family after her husband died. His father had trouble showing any emotions and never uttered the words, "I love you," to anyone in his household, especially his sons. His own father died when he was young, so he never really knew a father's love, making it hard to impossible for him to show emotions. He earned a living as a machinist and had a job at a local factory. He was known for being a very opinionated man, often arguing with friends and family members about everything from politics to sports. He was a decent provider but was so emotionally distant from his wife and his little boys that they felt disconnected from him.

The primary role he played was disciplinarian to his sons. There hung in the closet off the kitchen, on a large brass hook, a huge brown strap. The ends had been cut into strips just to make it more painful. That was the tool of choice used by Jessie when it came time to disciplining Trevor or his brother. Trevor would catch an ass whooping more often than his brother and the severity would vary depending more on Jessie's mood than the act. A fact that Trevor voiced more than once but which fell on deaf ears.

Everyone considered Trevor's father a well-read man because he wasn't afraid or timid when it came to telling people what they should do even though he had little to no experience on the subject. The reality was that he didn't read much other than the local newspaper.

Trevor's mother, Eva Marie Wills-Stillwell, was uber talented and creative but had no avenue for expression in her draconian marriage. For the most part, she was a stay-at-home mom that doted on her two little boys whowere the most important things in the world and he and his brother bathed in the glow of her love for them. Trevor had demonstrated some very unique uncanny abilities as a child, like advanced powers of observation. He also had almost a sixth sense when it came to interacting with and understanding people.

Eva Marie helped greatly in the development of Trevor's savant-like ability to evaluate and read situations and people. She helped him sharpen his talent and honed the skills he demonstrated because she thought it would be a useful skill no matter what he ended up doing, but especially if he chose a profession in law enforcement like her dad. There, his uncanny ability to size up situations and read people would prove invaluable. Trevor displayed this unique talent at an early age, and Eva decided to cultivate it any way she could.

One of the ways was by playing a game they called Operation: Watching You. If they were in a grocery or department store, Eva would pick a person for Trevor to watch. Trevor would watch the person, studying their movements, expressions, mannerisms, behavior and other miscellaneous elements. Then on the ride home, Eva would ask Trevor questions about the person. What did they do for a living, what kind of person was he or she? Trevor was expected to make an educated guess based on his observations and his unique abilities. Eva would always pick a person who she knew or knew a little about so she could measure the accuracy of Trevor's assertions and conclusions.

On one particular trip to Cartwright's Department Store, Trevor surprised and shocked Eva and inadvertently exposed a friend's dark secret. "Trevor, see that man with the yellow hat over there looking at the display?" Eva Marie was careful not to point at the man as she spoke gently into her ten-year-old son's ear.

Trevor smiled because he knew that the game was on. He was excited but calmly walked over to where the man was standing and pretended to be looking at the Mickey Mouse watch display. While the man was talking to a saleswoman, Trevor studied the man intently then something caught his attention. He noticed something on his face, then something about his right hand.

During the ride home, Trevor was uncharacteristically quiet. He sat stoically in the back seat of their car.

"Trevor, what's wrong baby?" Eva Marie asked as she looked at him through the rearview mirror.

"Mom, I think that man hurt someone, and it probably was a girl."

Eva Marie knew the man she had asked him to watch—he was the boyfriend of a friend of hers, but what she didn't know was that it was an abusive relationship. Until her little boy with the uncanny gift exposed the torrid aspects of their relationship.

"Why do you think he hurt someone Trevor?" Eva pulled the car over and turned to the back seat.

"Well, he had a cut on his cheek; it looked just like the cut that Joey had after his mother slapped him for cursing. Then I also noticed that he kept rubbing his hand and it looked bruised and swollen and then he asked the woman behind the counter if she thought the gift he was buying would be good as an apology." The pace of his speech was faster than normal. He was nervous and upset.

Trevor continued, "Mom, do you think he hurt someone?"

"Baby, don't worry about it, I'll take care of everything. I am very proud of you."

Trevor smiled at his mother. "Mom, can we not play that game anymore or for a while anyway?"

"Of course baby."

After that incident, Eva decided to find other ways to develop outlets for his talents.

Eva Marie was much young than their father, fifteen years his junior, and maybe that was why she could relate to her two young boys better than he could. She instilled in both her sons strong moral values, a sense of responsibility, and deep caring for others. She tried to instill in both her boys a strong moral fiber that would help them navigate the obstacles and challenges they would face in their lives.

Each December, she would take temporary work at a local department store because she wanted to make sure that her boys had the best Christmas possible. And she always succeeded in that regard; he and his brother would awake on Christmas morning to an abundance of toys stacked on the living room couch and chairs and under the Christmas tree. Without fail, he and his brother got everything that they asked for from Santa. Their doting mother made sure of that.

It wasn't until the façade of Santa faded when Trevor reached the age of twelve that he started noticing that money was a major issue in his household and his parents sometimes struggled to make ends meet. As the reality of his family's financial situation started to become clearer to him, his apartment daydream became more focused on asset acquisition. He started stocking up his imaginary apartment with the things he wanted that his parents didn't have and couldn't afford, things he had seen on TV or on display at the local department and electronic stores.

Case in point, the bedroom in his imaginary apartment had a brand new nineteen-inch Sony Trinitron with a matching Sony VCR just like the one he saw in the window of the local electronics store. His childhood reality was a ten-inch off-brand black-and-white TV with spotty reception and a rabbit ear antenna that had to be contorted every way possible in order to get a halfway decent picture. But almost every Saturday that beat-up old black and white TV became the centerpiece of he and his brother's universe, a cavalcade of unmatchable joy.

It started with the Saturday morning cartoon lineup which consisted mainly of Hanna-Barbera cartoons, shows like *The Banana Splits, Birdman and The Galaxy Trio, Moby Dick and Mighty Mightor, Space Ghost and Dino Boy, The Herculoids,* and *Sealab 2020.*

Cartoons were followed by *WWWF Championship Wrestling* with its exciting cast of colorful ethnic characters, like Chief Jay Strongbow, Bruno "The Living Legend" Sammartino, and

Ivan "The Polish Hammer" Putski. Each week the WWWF's stable of baby-face or good guy wrestlers would face off against the heels or bad guy wrestlers, which included the likes of "The Big Cat" Ernie Ladd, Stan "The Man" Stasiak, Stan "The Lariat" Hanson, and "King Kong" Bruiser Brody. The battles in the WWWF were very much like the conflicts between the heroes and villains of Marvel Comics that he and his brother loved so much.

He couldn't wait for a new heel or villain to enter WWWF territory. Their arrival was commonplace and they were introduced to the audience on the weekly TV show by entering the ring with one of the triumvirate of evil managers: Classy Freddie Blassie, the Grand Wizard of Wrestling, or Captain Lou Albano. After posing and strutting around the ring and yelling at the studio audience the heel would then proceed to thrash a jobber, one of a group of wrestlers whose role was to be cannon fodder and do the job of getting the heel over. At the end of the match the heel and his manager would bombastically claim they would end the reign of the champion, which for the majority of the 1960s and 70s was Bruno Sammartino, and later Bob Backlund. To his youthful mind this was entertainment at its best.

However, the coup de grâce of his Saturday TV love affair was the airing of the greatest TV show of all time: Channel 56's *Creature Double Feature*, which aired classic horror and monster movies starting at high noon. Classics like *Attack of the Mushroom People* and *War of the Gargantuas*. Next up was a late afternoon viewing of an amalgamation of reruns of some all-time great TV sci-fi shows and thrillers: *Kolchak: the Night Stalker*; *Space 1999*; *The Outer Limits*; and *The Avengers* with the super sexy Emma Peel. This cavalcade of TV shows concluded at 8:00 p.m. with another episode of the *Creature Feature*. On those special Saturdays where he could incorporate his Kelly's Hamburger, penny candy, and comic shop junket, the TV lineup transformed the day into pure nirvana.

Adjacent to the imaginary bedroom was the living room nestled in the center was a wrap-around black leather couch adorned with several red and gold throw pillows. At the front and to the sides of the couch were a set of rectangular coffee tables with glass tops and polished brass legs. A twenty-five-inch color Sony TV and a JVC hi-fi stereo set rounded out living room decor.

During his childhood, he and his brother would play their LPs and 45s on a ten-year-old record player that had two small speakers with a short in the wiring. While they listened to their records the sound would fade in and out like the police sirens as they raced through the neighborhood.

Moving from the living room into the dining room there stood a glass dining table with a brass outline and foundation that seated four. A large four-pronged cast-iron candleholder rested in the center of the table. A small but functional kitchenette was located off the dining room which housed all the amenities of a modern kitchen, including a dish washer and microwave—luxuries his parents could not afford and that his dad thought were wasteful and a poor use of his hard-earned, ever stretched, paycheck.

After all, Trevor's dad had two able-bodied dishwashers sleeping in the attic. Why would he ever need a machine to wash dishes when his sons were highly capable of performing that nightly task? Why did his father need a newfangled microwave oven; his wife was quite adept at keeping his dinner warm by using the conventional oven. His father was hard on him and his brother but loved them deeply even though he sometimes treated them like indentured servants.

There were other times when his dad showed how much he cared. When he was five years old his father worked the third shift at the Brown & Smith's Factory. Occasionally, he would wake up early enough to catch his dad arriving home, and more often than not his dad would greet him with a new comic book. Years later he would always fondly remember those early morning encounters with his dad.

Although The Apartment Daydream was specific and detailed down to the name brands of each item, at its core it portended a very simple desire: to have his own apartment that was his and his alone with very nice things in it. He was a realist and by the time he turned fifteen he knew that to bring his dream apartment to fruition there were only two distinct avenues open to him. A walk down easy street, where money grew on trees; or a long winding road full of sacrifice and hard work.

Most of his childhood friends had chosen the first option. A life of drug dealing could provide copious amounts of cash very quickly. More than enough to pay the rent on a spacious apartment and buy Sony Trinitrons galore, but he knew that lifestyle was not sustainable. It was fleeting and led inextricably to either an early grave or prison, neither of which he found appealing. So it would be the hard way for K. Trevor Stillwell.

It all came together for Trevor during his sixteenth year of life, that was when he came to the realization that The Apartment Daydream and possibly his future success would require him to make some radical changes in his life. He decided he had to leave the public high school he attended with all his neighborhood friends and enroll in Brentwood Christian Academy for Boys, where ninety percent of the graduates were accepted into college.

Trevor was so determined to make this change that he did so without consulting his parents. He decided to take the entrance exam and if he passed then he would tell them.

He also knew that the annual tuition would be a financial burden for his family, so he developed a plan to counteract cost-related objections that would undoubtedly be voiced by his father. He lined up a series of scholarships that included a partial scholarship for agreeing to play basketball for Brentwood and another from the NAACP if he maintained a 3.0 grade point average or higher. Any additional monetary shortfall he would make up for by working at the sporting goods warehouse of a Brentwood booster he met last summer while playing in a basketball tournament. He felt confident that if he was accepted, the cost of attending wouldn't derail his plan to attend Brentwood. What did concern Trevor was how his parents would react to his decision to leave his current high school to enroll in Brentwood without first consulting with them.

He was completely shocked by their reaction, or lack thereof. His father sat silently over his dinner plate and showed no outward reaction to the news, while his mother just smiled and looked at him glowingly. Her eyes full of a mother's pride. And that was it. Much to Trevor's surprise, they never talked about it again.

Trevor passed the entrance exam by the skin of his teeth. His high school guidance counselor infomed him that he passed by the smallest of margins; he wasn't surprised given the lack of education he received in the city's horrendous public school system. He moved from one grade to the next without learning much of anything. He couldn't remember ever doing any homework or taking many exams or tests. His time in junior high school at Bishop Bentley was a prime example of everything that was wrong with the public school system. Violence in the corridors and apathy in the classroom.

Trevor also found out that his Brentwood math test scores were far below an acceptable level but were somewhat offset by his proficiency in the reading and writing portions of the exam. Trevor knew that his abilities in those areas were mainly due to reading comic books and not his schooling. Although he didn't learn to read solely by reading comic books, he did advance his ability and reading comprehension level through

Marvel Comics. He would write down words he didn't know and look them up because he wanted to understand everything that was going on in a particular issue. During the late 1960s and early 1970s Marvel Comics recognized that many of its readers were college students and started writing more and more stories for that audience. Trevor was a beneficiary of Marvel's focus on more complex and detailed writing and storytelling. So, Trevor always attributed some of his success at Brentwood and later at Mathias College to the chief editor of Marvel Comics, Stan Lee, and his outstanding stable of writers.

His first year at Brentwood was his junior year of high school, and as he walked the hallowed corridors of the prestigious all-boys academy, he thought he was prepared for life at Brentwood. The reality was an eye-opening experience. He went from having no real homework to having three hours' worth each night and a test every week, as well as midterm exams and finals. Those first few weeks were tough. He thought about quitting but made the necessary adjustments. By October he had found his groove. Trevor started to excel in the classroom and finished his junior year at Brentwood Academy on the honor roll. He eventually graduated with a 3.3 GPA.

Although The Apartment Daydream had slowed and eventually stopped all together during his time at Brentwood, he never forgot it; it had left an indelible mark and there were always reminders. While in college he had to share a small two-bedroom apartment with four other students due to his limited financial resources. Stiffening his resolve and reminding him of the importance of that childhood daydream.

He was very proud of his academic achievements at Brentwood Academy as well as his success on the basketball court, but what he was equally proud of was that he resisted the siren call of the "streets." Pretty much all of Trevor's childhood friends had either dropped out of high school or rarely attended, instead choosing to earn the quick cash offered by the streets. Trevor was not immune to the temptation; he could feel the pull too. Most kids who grew up in the inner city felt the pull. The temptation was real and very enticing, but Trevor had refused to give into the allure of the fast cash, beautiful women, and lavish the lifestyle that came along, at least temporarily, with slinging dope and hustling.

During college he would go home on the weekends or during school vacations and see some of his old high school friends driving brand new cars, wearing the newest Adidas sweat suits with thick twenty-four-inch gold chains around their necks while flashing wads of hundred-dollar bills. On the surface, they seemed to be living large. Trevor was lucky to have twenty dollars in his pocket on a good day. He sometimes thought to himself that with his smarts, instincts, and ability to read people he could make a fortune and become a kingpin in the drug trade.

But he knew above all, he did not want to live his life profiting on human weakness. That would have been a violation of his moral code. This unspoken code was deeply embedded within him by his mother. She wasn't preachy but she knew right from wrong and instilled good values in her sons. A solid sense of what was right and what was wrong, and the knowledge that God was real and a part of their lives. Despite his own moral compass, he didn't look down on those who chose the street lifestyle or begrudge them for it. He believed that his morality was his and his alone. He never tried to impose his moral code on others. He felt that each person was responsible for their actions; therefore, it was up to the individual to decide where to draw the line for their own personal view of right and wrong.

AS TREVOR CLIMBED the old sturdy mahogany staircase to the third floor, he felt a sudden rush of adrenalin that caused his left hand to tremble slightly. Anxiously searching for the key, he checked the left pocket of his loose-fit tan khakis then the right. The rush reminded him of the Christmas mornings of his childhood. He was surprised at his reaction until he reflected on the moment and realized that this marked the attainment of the apartment of his dreams.

His thoughts were interrupted as his searching right hand stumbled across a small metal object in his right pocket. He clutched the key and inserted it gently into the circular lock. Before turning the key, he paused in quiet reflection.

Relishing a momentous occasion was nothing new to Trevor. When handed his college diploma from the dean of the Business School of Mathias College, he paused on stage for so long, basking in his moment of accomplishment, that the entire graduation procession came to a complete stop for several long, slightly awkward seconds.

With a sudden and swift turn of the key and a slight nudge from his free hand, the door slowly opened with a slight creak. The room was bathed in golden beams of afternoon sunlight which danced across the floorboards like a yellow strobe light across a dance floor. Trevor walked into the living room of his spacious apartment. It was the largest room in the apartment and the radiant sunlight that emanated from three large windows caused him to squint slightly. The hardwood floors cast colorful reflections from the sunlight and seemed to be heralding his accomplishment through a kaleidoscope of color and light.

As he approached the windows, Trevor cupped his right hand over his eyes to block the piercing brightness of the early afternoon sun. When he reached the center window, the largest of the three, the sunlight dissolved into the view of the bustling thoroughfare of Sassafras Avenue.

A smiled engulfed Trevor's lean, angular face as he opened the window wide enough to sit along the sill and gaze down on the busy street. Trevor was a handsome, well-built twenty-three-year-old black man. He had dark thick eyebrows, long eyelashes, and light brown eyes. His curly black hair was cut short and tapered on the sides. He stood at six feet five and had an athletic build: wide shoulders, long muscular arms, and thin but sinewy legs. He looked around his first apartment and smiled. This was indeed all he imaged it would be and more. *Finally!* he thought to himself.

Sassafras Avenue was teeming with life. People of all of colors, race, and creeds wore grooves into its well-traveled pavement, interacting and congregating along its open palm. The street was situated in a historically African American neighborhood which suffered from the effects of poverty and crime, but over the last decade it had undergone a remarkable transformation. One that dramatically changed the racial composition, economics, and quality of life in the neighborhood.

The neighborhood metamorphosis started slowly but the results were undeniable. It began with a group of people who were attracted to the area because of its eclectic housing mix and urban setting. Brownstones and townhouses of all shapes and sizes rested along the sidewalks of Sassafras. Young white professionals looking for urban-centric living experience, and artists and students who were attracted by the ornate architecture of the brownstones, the affordable rent, and its proximity to the downtown area and Longfellow City College which had received national acclaim for its Liberal Arts and Contemporary Music curriculums.

Soon word started to spread about something special happening on and around Sassafras, but really no one knew for sure what was to come. New faces popped up seemingly every day, and as more people started to take up residence there, market forces quickly came into play. The increasing demand for this "funky" living space eventually caught the eye of deep-pocketed developers throughout the state who started buying up many of the residential and mixed-use buildings.

They renovated the brownstones and townhouses into creative work/live apartments, loft apartments, and studio apartments. As the quality of housing stock improved and demand continued to rise, local business owners and fledging entrepreneurs were quick to seize the opportunity that this population surge represented.

Previously abandoned storefronts were rehabbed and reinvented as unique specialty shops, unique handcrafted gift boutiques and quaint little supper clubs. All of a sudden there was a unique vibrancy to the area. Street vendor stands and carts started to dot the streetscape—selling everything from exotic incense and candles to high-end kitchen wares. The artisans, as they came to be known, quickly established themselves as the lifeblood of the street, giving it a unique character and feel found nowhere else in the city.

The last major catalyst of transition and rebirth for the neighborhood was ushered in by a group of people given the moniker of "New Landers" because they were viewed as being new to the country as well as the neighborhood. These immigrants, rich in their individual cultures and steeped in the spirit of entrepreneurism, started conducting business on the strip. Most of them lived in other parts of the city but made a daily migration to the area to sell their wares and conduct commerce on Sassafras and its network of interconnecting streets. They either relocated their existing businesses or opened entirely new ones. Small storefronts on Sassafras were sometimes sub-divided into smaller storefronts. These stores displayed exotic imports from their native lands—the islands of the Caribbean and West Africa. Soon their brightly lit storefronts and colorful vendor stands dotted the streetscape like fireflies on a southern autumn night. During this time of transition, the wind of change blew often. A new Indian, Southeast Asian, or other culturally enriched storefront or restaurant would sprout on the fertile ground of Sassafras and its network of smaller side streets, intertwining their sumptuous smells and rich culture, creating an atmosphere as unique as it was accessible.

The eclectic mix of people, ideas, and tastes attracted visitors from throughout the state and became a major tourist attraction. A place once known for despair, poverty, and crime was transformed into a destination, a place where the hippest people wanted to live, shop, and play. Specialty boutiques, trinket shops, and art galleries were comfortably nestled alongside coffee shops where a young would-be artist could recite homespun poetry or strum out heartfelt tunes until the early morning hours. The pulse of the street was palpable, and Trevor was excited to be living in its midst.

Trevor was about to move away from the window to take in the rest of his new apartment when he noticed three young black kids joking with one another outside the neighborhood record store, Funky Beats. They were laughing and pointing at one of the kids in the group who seemed to be taking the brunt of their laughter.

It reminded Trevor of the times he and his friends would crack jokes on each other after school while waiting for the girls from St. Anne's to walk by on their way to the city bus depot. Spending the last two years of high school at Brentwood's all-boys academy sure made him appreciate female anatomy. The bell that signified the end of the school day was analogous to the starting gun of a race; a hormone-laced race to the down city bus stop where the sight of young nubile legs protruding from plaid skirts was the centerpiece of Trevor's after-school day.

His eyes moved to the corner, where amid a group of people at the intersection, he noticed a woman walking diagonally across the street toward his building. She was easy to spot. Her brilliantly colored summer dress swayed gently around her body as a light afternoon breeze stirred. As the breeze gained momentum, the dress gently enveloped the contour of her sexy form like a lover's passionate embrace. Trevor could see the delicate lines and curves of her mocha-colored body.

He exhaled deeply. "Oh, my Lord! The girls from St. Anne's never looked like that."

Her syncopated walked gave the appearance that her hips were moving to a sensual rhythm that resonated through her body. Her full, round breasts rested softly against the silky fabric of her dress. She stepped from the street to the side-walk, heading directly for the entrance of the Hillcrest Apart-ments. *Does she live here?* The thought brought a rush of excite-ment. Should he race downstairs and try to meet her? Was there enough time to intercept her? He glanced down as she ascended the steps and disappeared into his building.

That warm, familiar feeling swelled within him and he found himself secretly hoping that she lived within the walls of the Hillcrest and that one day he would find himself slowly undressing her, gently slipping her underpants down her hips and over her thighs. Embracing her chest to chest and tasting the flavor of her rich mocha-colored skin.

Despite his vivid imagination and predilection for flights of sexual fancy, Trevor was a cautious man when it came to trying to satisfy his prodigious sexual desires. Like most men he hated using rubbers—he thought it took away from the full sexual experience, greatly lessening his and the woman's enjoyment—so he never used them. However, he offset this risky sexual behavior by being very circumspect and selective about whom he slept with. He didn't sleep with every girl who gave him some rhythm. Or if a girl had a rep for sleeping around, he wouldn't mess with her. It wasn't a perfect method but it had worked for him.

Also, although he loved beautiful women, he had learned early in life that most beautiful women were very troubled with longstanding confounding issues and carried enough baggage to destroy any chance of a drama free relationship. Yes, contrary to popular belief, beautiful women carried more than their fair share of issues, hang-ups, and insecurities, which all too often manifested themselves in their relationships.

After the woman had entered the building, Trevor continued to gaze out of the window, seemingly transfixed on the mass of people as they went about their business. A nondescript white woman with blond hair argued with a man outside a bar a few storefronts down from Funky Beats. She was stumbling, trying to keep from completely losing her balance as she circled him, jabbing her finger close to his face. She got too close and poked him below the right eye. He grabbed his face, turned abruptly and walked toward a side street adjacent to the bar. She stood there for several minutes, seemingly unaware that the object of her tirade had departed. Uncertain of what to do next, she waved her hand in the air, as if dismissing him, and retreated into the bar.

BEEEEP! A HORN blared loudly, attracting Trevor's attention away from the bar to a cream-colored convertible sedan moving slowly with the top down. It stopped at the intersection of Morgan Street and Sassafras Avenue. A fiercely dark-complexioned man, wearing a brown fedora and oversized sunglasses, propped himself up in the driver's seat of the car and shouted, "So fine, girl you so fine I'd tell where da slaves is hidin' for a minute of your time! Damn girl!" A broad but menacing smile engulfed his face.

"Serious girl, you know who I is, right, and what I can do for ya, right? Come on now, don't play games wit' me now!" Trevor strained to hear the man's voice. "...you know you can be livin' large, just axe your girl, she tell ya..." Trevor struggled to make out the man's words because as soon as they left his darkened lips, they seemed to be swallowed by the cacophony of sound emanating from the crowded street.

Trevor couldn't see the man clearly either. Besides being obscured by the brim of his hat, his face was so dark that his facial features seemed to be swallowed in a void of his darkness; it was like looking into a shadow. Maybe it was his featureless face, menacing grin, or his aggressive tone—Trevor wasn't quite sure—but there was something about the man that caused an uneasy feeling in his gut. He never liked overly demonstrative or loud people, especially those who verbally assaulted women, but there was something more to dislike about this man, something that he was certain of.

Despite the featureless man's best attempts to engage the woman in conversation, she was unfazed by his boisterous overtures and did not break stride or acknowledge his presence. *He was dead right though*, Trevor thought to himself. She was as fine and as sexually desirable as a woman could be. Her caramel brown skin glistened in the sunlight. Her straight jet-black hair flowed across her shoulders and down her tight-fitting yellow blouse. Her lean but thick stomach was exposed two inches above and below her pierced navel. Her cut-off jean shorts left little to the imagination. Even from Trevor's heightened vantage point, there was no way to ignore her perfect crescent; that place on her body where her lower buttock flowed into the back of her thigh. It was a sight that would surely weaken even the most devoted of men.

Each step she took, every movement of her body, accentuated her raw sexual energy. Trevor knew that a woman who embodied that amount of sexuality was surely a harbinger of trouble. Was she worth all the conflict and chaos that would surely follow? He had developed an axiom which he knew had been proven tried and true: The more beautiful a woman was, the more problems, issues, and drama she had in her life. Trevor liked to say that beautiful women tended to carry backpacks where they would accumulate unresolved issues and carry them from relationship to relationship. Never resolving any; just carrying them into each new relationship.

But she was so very beautiful, and he thought of all the things he would like to do to her and with her. He decided right then and there if the opportunity presented itself, he would throw all caution to the wind and take a chance with her. Her beauty and sexuality were that intoxicating. He couldn't seem to take his eyes off her. *Thank God for Daisy Dukes*, he thought, and smiled.

He was never a fan of the *Dukes of Hazard*—that TV series was much too country for his taste—but Catherine Bach in those tight high-cut shorts was a sight to behold, especially for a boy of twelve with raging hormones. As was Thelma from *Good Times* with her skintight jeans.

He felt that warm flow within him. A feeling that always accompanied thoughts of beautiful women. Slowly, his mind drifted into thoughts about some of the beautiful women of his past. He thought of Lisa, how she would moan ever so slightly when he kissed her inner thigh; and of Pam doing her sexy little dance for him in her underwear; and Monique's soft lips resting against his cheek as she slept. Those joyous thoughts slowly dissolved into the harsh reality of the pain and the indelible scars left by the women of his past. Sometimes it was the pain of unrequited love, others the product of unmet expectations, and still others of unchecked hubris.

The horn sounded loudly again, abruptly interrupting Trevor's daydream, although this time the sound emanated from directly below his window. Again, it was the featureless man in the cream-colored sedan.

"Dis' is a nice place to live, ain't it girl? I'm sure it doesn't come cheap!" Trevor could now clearly make out the man's words and the steely and ominous tone that accompanied them.

"Oh, you cain't speak today, dat's au'ight girl, but I think you may be changin' your mind soon. I be seein' you 'round da way girl, real soon you heard!" His words hung in the air like clouds on an overcast day as the car turned sharply and accelerated away from the sidewalk.

Trevor watched as his car sped down Sassafras Avenue. He looked down, expecting to see her again, but she had made her way through the door and into the Hillcrest before he could get another glimpse of her stunning beauty or gauge her reaction to the shadow man's last few words.

PATRONS CROWDED THE sidewalk and occupied all of the small oval-shaped, olive green plastic tables scattered in front of Sal's Pizza Emporium. The way the tables and chairs were scattered along the sidewalk reminded him of how his brother would keep his side of their bedroom. Such disorganization bothered Trevor to no end. He preferred all things to be organized, neat and orderly like his sweaters in the milk crates, but his experiences had taught him that most people did not look at things through his structured prism. So, he held his compulsive desire to start straightening out the tables and chairs at bay and entered Sal's.

It was hot inside the little pizza parlor. The heat generated by Sal's large silver ovens hug unforgivingly in the air. The large wooden ceiling fans only managed to push the hot smothering air from one place to another like rearranging pillows on a crowded bed. Trevor quickly realized it would be impossible to enjoy a slice of pizza while sitting at a booth inside Sal's, so he decided to sit outside in the cordoned-off section of sidewalk and started jockeying for one of those olive green plastic tables. He stood and looked around and realized that although all the tables were taken, he was the only person waiting for one to open up.

A slender black man in a tightfitting sharkskin suit walked by and acknowledged Trevor. "What up, partner?'

"Nothing much," replied Trevor. As he watched the man pass by and then cross the street, his thoughts drifted to the past when he and his pals would hang at the park and watch the street hustlers and drug dealers who congregated there playing dominos and shooting dice.

Trevor, like most kids growing up in the projects, admired their stylish threads, flashy cars, and gaudy jewelry, but what most impressed Trevor was the sheer volume of fine women that seemed to fawn over their every move. A young Trevor and his friends tried to emulate the rhythmic way they walked and copy their creative street vernacular. To Trevor it was an almost scientific use of body language. He remembered watching each hustler posing against the walls of The Mose while spinning tales of women, money, and personal conquests. Each story more bombastic than the last; each hustler seeming more demonstrative than the next, strutting like peacocks on parade along the tattered concrete of the Mosley Street Park.

Trevor spent most of his time while attending the Bishop Bentley Junior High School skipping out at lunch and spending the afternoon hanging with the other truants at The Mose, as it was commonly called. It was the largest recreational park in the city and always in a constant state of disrepair. In the playground area the slides were the only things still intact and in working order. The basketball courts had bent rusted rims with no nets and two-inch-wide cracks in the pavement that made dribbling the ball not only challenging but hazardous. More than a few twisted and sprained knees and ankles were the result of a newcomer to the park trying to dribble quickly up court without knowing the lay of the land. Adjacent to the courts was a diamond-shaped softball field that looked more like a trash dump—filled with discarded furniture, waist high in weeds—than a field of athletic endeavor.

The park was surrounded on all sides by rundown public housing and dilapidated and vacant storefronts, but despite its condition The Mose was an oasis of sorts for the neighborhood kids or at least as close to one as the ghetto could offer. You could find everything at The Mose—gambling, girls, drugs; it was a hustlers' paradise.

Trevor and his friends were serial truants, spending many mornings and almost every afternoon at The Mose when they should have been in class. They would shoot craps for a few hours, smoke some weed, then go shoot some hoops. The old men who hung on the periphery of the park playing cards and dominos would bring coolers filled with beer and sit them on the nearby park benches. Easy pickings for Trevor's crew.

Trevor and his friends would take the beer and set up shop on the smallest of the three basketball courts, situated on a grassy embankment, the top court overlooked the entirety of The Mose. This bird's eye view allowed them to see everything that transpired at The Mose, including their all-time favorite voyeuristic activity watching the hustlers run their street game on some unwitting victim who happened to wander into their lair or some new customer who was trying to buy some drugs.

There was a time when having a stable of fine women, a truck load of easy money and a jet-black Beamer were Trevor's only aspirations. And if not for a simple daydream about an apartment and desire to succeed in life, he might have taken that easy path and been swallowed by the streets. Instead, he chose to leave the underachieving public high school and eschew hanging in The Mose for the Brentwood Christian Academy for Boys and three hours of homework per night.

So much evolved from that fateful evening at dinner when he announced to his parents that he had passed the entrance exam and was going to Brentwood Christian Academy for Boys. declaring he wanted to go to college and that it was obvious to him that if he continued on his present educational track that there was no way that college would be an option which was followed by his parents' silent acquiescence.

His time at Brentwood was as much of a life-altering experience as he imagined. During his first week there, a teammate on the basketball team suggested he take a class on black literature because it was supposed to be an easy grade for any black student. His teammate Roy's exact words were, "Yo, it's taught by a black man and if you're black it is an easy grade; all you have to do is attend the class. I am telling you Trev, man. And with as much coursework as they give you here at Brentwood, you're going to need as many easy A's as possible."

The black teacher's name was Ezekiel Harris. He was an intimidating presence at six feet six and close to three hundred pounds. He played pro basketball in Spain after a stellar career at Mathais College.

Between the constant truancy and the apathy of most of the teachers he had encountered during his time in the city's public schools, Trevor didn't know much about black history and almost nothing about black literature. His experience of black characterizations in books was limited to the black superheroes of Marvel Comics like Luke Cage, a.k.a. Power Man, and the Black Panther, so even though Roy was insistent that the class was a sure shot, Trevor was leery.

And his skepticism was well warranted, the class was no easy grade. Mr. Harris was not only physically imposing, he was very intelligent and a fiercely proud black man who not only didn't make it easy for his black students, he held the bar higher for them. He understood the challenges they faced, and would face, growing up black in America and he was committed to helping them maximize their potential and develop a sense of self-awareness and self-worth by exposing them to black literature. This class was no easy A. Yet Trevor excelled; he was intrigued and inspired by Mr. Harris's class.

Under Mr. Harris's tutelage, Trevor studied the works of James Baldwin, Ralph Ellison, and Richard Wright. These writers opened Trevor's eyes to the reality of ghetto life. Their writings reinforced the desire within him to rise above the false dreams of ghetto fame and materialism. Their works exposed the grim underbelly of racism in a way he hadn't thought of before. Lifting the veil and exposing the strings, through the prism of their writings he could see how the puppet master's tools of systemic racism, structural poverty, and social injustice manipulated the lives of not just black people, but all disenfranchised people.

He began to view the hustlers at The Mose in an entirely different light, as pawns in society's game of oppression, ignorance, and poverty. Armed with this new enlightenment, and driven by Mr. Harris's inspirational and motivational lectures, he dove into his studies and developed a ferocious hunger for knowledge.

Getting good grades didn't come easy for him; academic achievement was a struggle at first because he was so far behind his peers at Brentwood. All of them had received the best educations from the best schools that money could buy since kindergarten.

Through concentration, determination, and laser-like focus, he achieved academic excellence. He excelled on the basketball court too, earning third place All-State honors by averaging eighteen points per game, eight rebounds, and eight assists. By the end of his senior year, his GPA put him in the twentieth percentile of his class. Coupled with a stellar year on the basketball court, Trevor had several college scholarship offers.

What really separated Trevor from the norm was that, unlike most other successful black students at the prestigious school with similar socioeconomic backgrounds, he achieved academic excellence without divesting himself of his neighborhood or the childhood friends who had helped shape and define him. Sure, he didn't go the local public high school with his friends or hang out at The Mose during the school year, but the works of those writers that Mr. Harris had introduced him to spoke about taking from the street only those things that were advantageous and leaving all the negative stuff behind. How Trevor interpreted that was not everything that he experienced hanging in the streets and The Mose was negative and needed to be purged. Some of his experiences had a redeeming value that would help him later in life.

During his time running the streets with his friends, Trevor had gained an innate understanding of their inner workings. When added to his already solidified ability to read situations and people, Trevor was confident that he had a formidable set of unique skills when it came to dealing with people or difficult situations. He knew how to survive and even prosper without being absorbed or corrupted by them. He knew the street hustle. He learned about the art of manipulation and subterfuge. He could run a con game with the best of them and, more importantly, recognize when one was being run on him or others. He developed almost a sixth sense when it came to assessing people and understanding the complexities of human nature and social interactions. He had developed a talent for this inexact science.

It was a common occurrence from grade school on that whenever a friend found himself in a tight spot that required more brains than brawn, they sought out Trevor. He developed an innate ability to resolve combustible situations without much, if any, collateral damage because of his ability to intuit the issues of a situation and quickly read a person's motives and rationale. He could analyze a situation and figure out what a person valued and then use that to negotiate and defuse or resolve the problem.

This was a skill that was equal parts birthright and equal parts learned, developed, enhanced and sharpened on the street dealing with the hustlers, pimps, and drug couriers in his neighborhood. He would listen to the way they spoke and read their body language in order to make a spot-on judgment about their character. He prided himself on his ability to read people. There was nothing psychic or supernatural about it. It was the direct result of learning to survive the streets. And unlike most of his classmates, Trevor was equally comfortable in a college lecture hall as he was on the corner of Lexington and Martin Luther King Boulevard.

A **WOMAN GENTLY BRUSHED** against his extended knee as she passed. "Excuse me," she said in a soft voice as she hurried by.

"No problem beautiful," Trevor said instinctively. Some women take offense to the use of such flowery comments from a stranger, but Trevor had a naturally disarming way about him that assuaged most of those concerns.

As she reached for the door, she turned and gently smiled at him. She was petite, about five feet four, but shapely and sexy. She had compelling topaz eyes and a lovely tawny complexion. In a word: Stunning. In the last few hours, Trevor had seen three of the most attractive and desirable women he had ever set eyes on. There was something unsettling about that, but he quickly dismissed it as good fortune.

"Thank you for the compliment, but I don't feel very pretty in this heat," she said as she glanced Trevor's way.

The outline of her body was reminiscent of an hourglass. Her round sturdy breasts perfectly complimented her slight fame, while her slender waistline gave way to supple hips. Trevor couldn't help but imagine his hands firmly guiding her hips in a spontaneous dance of passion.

"If you think it's hot out here, then you don't want to go in there." Trevor's words flowed smoothly from his lips as he tried to clear his mind of all carnal thoughts.

She stopped, holding the door ajar. "Don't tell me Sal's AC is on the fritz again?" she said sarcastically.

"I don't know, this is my first time here, but it seems so." Trevor shrugged his shoulders as he spoke.

She stood indecisively. She seemed to be struggling with what to do next. Trevor tried not to stare but her beauty entranced him.

"I've been waiting here for a table to open, but I'd be happy to give you the first one that becomes available," Trevor said, hoping that she'd accept.

"No, that's alright I be—" Before she could finish Trevor interrupted her.

"Or maybe we could share the next table, if that's alright with you?" She looked inquisitively at Trevor for a moment then looked around at the scattering of small plastic tables. A couple stood and motioned to Trevor that they were leaving.

"There's a free table, but if you don't want company I'll understand. It's all yours. No strings attached." Trevor showed no hint of the impending disappointment he would surely feel if she decided to sit alone.

A man exited the pizza shop, forcing her to relinquish her grip on the door handle, and she moved to the side of the entranceway. She hesitated as her eyes locked with Trevor's. The warmth of his wide brown eyes seemed to momentarily melt away her apprehension.

"No...no, that's okay. I'll share it with you, but I won't be here for long, I only came for a quick bite. I have to get to work soon." Despite Trevor's disarming approach and natural charm, she was noticeably uneasy.

Uneasy about what? he thought to himself.

"That cool. How 'bout you get the table and I'll order the food. What are you having?" Trevor asked.

"Oh, that won't be necessary. I can get my own," she replied sharply. It was clear to Trevor that breaking the ice with this exceptionally beautiful woman would be much more challenging than he expected.

SHE SAT AT the table engulfed by a cloud of uncomfortable silence that seemed to be emanating from deep inside her soul. Since returning to the table with their food, she had not looked directly at him or spoken a word. Instead, she focused her gaze downward or nervously stared over his left shoulder toward the street.

She was completely lost in her own thoughts and seemed to be carrying the worries of the world on her shoulders. Trevor realized that playing the aggressor probably wouldn't be the right move, so he decided to join her in silence and by doing so see if he could get her to relax and start to open up a bit.

But after another two minutes of awkward silence, he realized that here was a deeply troubled woman; the anxiety she exuded was palpable. He couldn't put his finger on it, but there was something very disconcerting about her silence. Then all of a sudden, like finding the answer to a crossword puzzle question, Trevor knew what it was she was feeling: FEAR! This beautifully captivating woman sitting across from him felt an intense fear and dread. Was it about something or someone?

He instinctively wanted to help, but he also understood that women were mercurial creatures and that this initial contact between them would go a long way to determining the outcome of their relationship. He was torn between his desire to help her regardless of the cost and his equally strong desire to feel her naked body glistening with sweat against his.

He knew that they were divergent paths because if he aggressively tried to help her with whatever situation she was facing, it most likely would impact his chances of getting with her, particularly if his help was viewed as selfish or unwanted interference, or somehow made things worse for her. He also understood that women placed an inordinate amount of value on their first impressions, much more so than a man.

Most women could determine within ten minutes of meeting a man whether he had a chance to get some or not. And once a woman makes that determination then it's pretty much set in stone. She reaches a verdict on whether she's going to give it up completely in a vacuum state; she needs no input other than that which she gathers during that first contact.

The details may change but the scenario is always the same. A man encounters a beautiful woman. He approaches her and starts to make conversation—run his game. She quickly assesses the probabilities. Like a computer, she processes the input data: his smile and physique, how he is dressed, his mannerisms and other miscellaneous and somewhat superficial characteristics, like the shoes he is wearing for example.

Conclusion reached: he can get it or he can't. It's that simple. The woman sets no timetable; it could happen later that night or a year from then. But one thing is for sure: the man is completely unaware that his fate has been predetermined before the end of that first conversation.

The mercurial nature of women is always in play because once a woman gives a man the "mental green light," he must be very careful not to say or do anything to cause her to change her mind, because she can and will at a moment's notice. A man can very easily talk his way right out of her panties and not even know it.

"Damn Trevor, remember that fine girl I stepped to at the

gas station the other day? You know; the one with long purple fingernails? She seemed like she was with it but I've called her a few times and she hasn't returned any of my calls."

What Trevor's friend Raja experienced that day was a woman changing from green light to red within the course of an initial conversation. Raja probably said too much or said the wrong thing or maybe she glanced down at his shoes and found them disagreeable. Whatever the case, he went from getting her number to an unanswered phone. She changed her mind within the initial ten minutes of their first encounter. He was not going to get the panties after all. The worst part, at least in Trevor's mind, was that Raja was completely oblivious to what had transpired. He thought the girl just flaked on him, but Trevor knew the truth.

With this woman sitting in front of him, Trevor knew he would have to tread very lightly given her agitated state of being. It was not the time for aggressive conversation. He wanted her to feel in control of their encounter, which he hoped would slowly loosen her up enough for him to eventually—kick his game.

A few more minutes passed, still no words were exchanged. In fact, she had barely taken a bite of her pizza. She just sat stoically, sipping on the straw of her diet Coke.

He noticed that she was becoming more visibly uncomfortable, nervously wiggling her leg back and forth. The table lurching slightly with every sway of her leg. Suddenly she tilted her head and started to scan the streetscape from left to right as if someone had called her name. She was definitely on edge; this sense of intense uneasiness seemed to be working toward a crescendo. He would have to take some action—risking it all in order to break the grip of tension that was emanating from her and starting to engulf him.

He panicked and, very uncharacteristically, he said the first thing that popped into his head. "So, do you live 'round here?"

She looked at him quickly. His question startled her. As though she had forgotten he was sitting at the table with her. It was the first time their eyes met since she was holding open the door to Sal's. Her topaz eyes were consumed with a deep concern and she struggled to answer.

"I...I live down the street a way, at the Hillcrest." She immediately regretted providing those specifics and quickly looked down, refocusing her gaze on the plastic tabletop.

He tried to hide his surprise, but his eyes widened with anticipation. "The Hillcrest huh, well, it looks like a nice place to live."

"You know what they say, looks can be deceiving," she said in a slightly sarcastic tone which seemed to mask her uneasiness for a moment.

"What do you mean; it's not a nice place to live?" Now Trevor was curious and eagerly awaited her reply.

"No, no, I...never mind, I really don't want to talk about it, besides I have to go or I'll be late for work." She stood quickly with her soda in hand.

"Hey, I'm sorry if I said something to upset you," Trevor pleaded. "No...you...you didn't, I just have to go," she replied hastily, and she turned to leave.

Trevor instinctively reached across the table and gently grabbed her arm. "Listen, I just got the keys this morning to my apartment at the Hillcrest. I wanted to know what living there was like, that's the only reason I asked." He quickly released her arm once he realized that he had grabbed it.

She stumbled a bit then stopped abruptly as if she had encountered an obstacle in her path. "You are going to be living at the Hillcrest?" she asked in an incredulous tone.

"Yeah, just saw the apartment this morning," he replied, somewhat perplexed by her reaction.

"Really, what apartment?" she questioned, somewhat disbelievingly.

"Apartment 3A," Trevor replied.

"That was Sherry's old apartment," she said softly as if speaking to herself.

"Really? Was she a friend of yours?"

"She was my best friend," she replied as if she was in a trance.

"Was?"

Before the word was out of his mouth, he regretted saying it. His mother always told him he'd make a great detective because he was such an inquisitive child, always searching for answers to questions about things he didn't understand or that intrigued him. Not much had changed over the years, he was still naturally curious. He couldn't seem to help it, but he knew this personality trait sometimes rubbed people the wrong way.

She slumped her shoulders slightly. "I mean...she's...she's still my friend...I think...it's just that I haven't seen her in a while." She was extremely hurt; it was as obvious to Trevor as her enduring beauty.

"What happened to her? Where is she now?" He figured that since he had started down this road the least he could do was try to satisfy his curiosity by asking some pointed questions.

"I don't know. She disappeared," she said as she shook her head slowly from side to side. With that she turned abruptly and walked to the corner of the storefront, disposed her uneaten pizza in the trash receptacle. With soda in hand she looked back at Trevor and tried to smile, but all she could muster was a half grin.

Trevor stood. "Maybe I'll see you around the Hillcrest?"

"You won't be easy to miss. You are the only man living at the Hillcrest." She turned and walked briskly down the street, disappearing behind a crowd of people gathered at the crosswalk.

Several minutes passed before Trevor realized they hadn't even exchanged names. As he sat and finished his food, he couldn't help but wonder what could possibly make such a beautiful woman so uneasy. What burden was she carrying? Trevor thought he felt a mutual attraction, at least initially, but her preoccupation with whatever was troubling her dimmed that sparkle in her eye. Maybe she had a man and was worried that he or one of his friends would see her having lunch with him? *Yeah, that's it.* It sounded reasonable, but Trevor's intuition was telling him that it wasn't quite that simple. The more he thought about her and how profoundly sad she was, the more Trevor changed gears from a man interested in her for her look and body to a man interested in helping a troubled woman.

It was the classic "Damsel Complex." At least that's how his best friend Rico Cubberson referred to it, and despite Trevor's assertions to the contrary, he had a hard time proving Rico wrong. Reflecting back, the Damsel Complex manifested itself in Trevor at a very early age.

When Trevor was ten years old, he helped a little girl named Jasmine, who lived next door, escape an abusive household by sneaking her into the basement of his house. She lived there for almost three weeks. Trevor would bring her food; he set up a cot for her to sleep on with plenty of blankets and her favorite books so she could pass the time. That lasted until Trevor's mother started to get suspicious about Trevor spending so much time in the basement. He covered his tracks by telling his mother that he was setting up some space with shelves in the basement to store his comic books.

Eventually, his mother stumbled upon the girl's basement hideaway while looking for a box of clothing to donate to the Salvation Army. She had a long talk with Trevor about the right and the wrong way to help someone. Contacting the proper authorities would have been the right way to help Jasmine. Hiding her in their basement was only a temporary solution. She didn't admonish him for what he did because he was trying to help someone who was in need. She was just trying to get him to think of the big picture solutions and not to rely on snap decisions that are inherently shortsighted. It proved to be a good lesson for Trevor.

When forced to confront it, he thought of it as a simple case of a young man having a caring heart. He wondered if the girl with the topaz eyes would be the next iteration of his Damsel Complex.

TREVOR WAS PUTTING in some kitchen items when he heard a resounding crash. He quickly darted into the living room. "Damn Rico! I hope that wasn't the box with those funky wineglasses I just bought from Pier 1," Trevor said disgustedly.

The big man exhaled heavily and bent over to retrieve the fallen box. "Nah, Trev; dis box is marked bedroom, so it's just full of lotion and dirty magazines to occupy your long lonely nights." Rico wasn't fat as much as he was round. His stomach was fairly small for a man of his size, but the outline of his body was circular. His arms, when relaxed by his sides, were propped up by the roundness of his frame.

"Yeah, right! That's your favorite hobby big man, not mine. Just be careful with my stuff. I think that box has all my smell-goods in it and if you broke my new bottle of Polo, man... you're all done. Besides, your big ass shouldn't be dropping a box that small anyway," Trevor said with a halfhearted smile.

"It's not the size of the box, Trev. It's those damn stairs that's wearing my ass out. Why you pick the weekend when the elevator broke?" Rico was sweating profusely as he spoke.

Trevor pointed in the direction of the bathroom and barked, "Damn Rico! Go get a towel and wipe your sweat off before you soak my floor."

"Sweatin' good for me Trev, my doctor told me that sweating

is the best way to lose weight. See, most of my weight is water weight." That comment brought a big smile to Trevor's face.

Rico responded to Trevor's wry smile. "Serious Trev, I lost thirty pounds simply by sweating out some water weight. I just sat in a steam room and the pounds came sweating off." Rico grabbed a towel from the linen closet in the bathroom.

"You really lost thirty pounds? From where Rico?"

"Stop messin' wit me Trev, I'm serious. I'm down to 280 kid," Rico said with a sense of pride.

"Really!" Trevor seemed genuinely impressed.

"Uh huh, for real, and if I keep hanging around dis place, I'll be down to a svelte two-forty in no time. Dis place is definitely motivatin' a brotha."

"Svelte? From slovenly to svelte in only a few weeks? Okay, if you say so Rico, and if my stairs are helping you, by all means, feel free to come climb them anytime you want big man."

"Naa man, it's not just da stairs. It's all these fine ass females in dis place. I mean, all morning I've seen nothin' but some fine ass females up in here. Make a brotha want to drop some serious poundage. You know what I mean?"

Rico continued, "And stop tripin', I'm not slovenly, man. I told you my room at my mom's is only a mess because I don't have enough room. If I had a nice apartment like dis place it would be spotless twenty-four seven."

Trevor smiled broadly again. "You're a trip Rico, but you're my boy. And I know what you mean. I've seen nothing but beautiful women coming and going in this place since I first walked in here and believe it or not, I think that I'm the only man living in the entire complex...well, other than this weird older guy who I think lives in the basement. He must be the apartment manager, or janitor or something. He's always wearing these ugly worn-out jean overalls."

"Why's he weird...because of his old overalls? Not everyone can be GQ Trevor."

Trevor looked disapprovingly at Rico. "Yo Rico, it's not just his overalls, man. I've seen him a few times and said 'what's up' to him but he doesn't say anything. He just looks at me like I got two heads or something."

"Maybe now he knows he's got some competition for the attention of all dese females now. He's probably feelin' da heat." Rico raised his eyebrows in an exaggerated fashion.

"Yeah, well, whatever the case. He better stop with the hard stare, or—"

Rico quickly interrupted him. "Or what Trev? What you gonna do? You got this dope crib. You start a crazy nice job in a week. You gonna take his head off and blow everything you've worked for? What's Bruce starting to rub off on you after all dese years or somethin'?" Rico shook his head and looked disappointedly at Trevor.

"Whatever man." Trevor waved him off and continued unpacking.

"See, like my great grand pappy usta say: You can take da black man out of the ghetto but you can't—"

"Yeah, yeah, yeah, I know Rico, I know." They looked at each other for a moment then both broke out in deep hearty laughter.

"Forget that janitor Trev, you one lucky brotha! You found da honey pot here. Check this: when I was carrying your case of lotion upstairs, I ran into one of the most beautiful females ever. I think she said her name was Sherry. Like the wine, and trust me she was fine as wine too."

Trevor, who had started removing a vase adorned with simulated Egyptian artwork from its padded box, stopped abruptly. "You met a girl named Sherry! Here in the Hillcrest?" He felt the vase slip from his grasp but quickly secured it with both hands.

"Come to think of it, I think her name was Sharon! Sherry! Sharon! What difference does it make? You know how I am wit

41

names; anyway she was fine as all and dat's all dat matters!" Rico exclaimed.

"Was it Sherry or Sharon, Rico? Simple question. And about that comment you made earlier. Between the two of us I think we both know who sits home alone and plays with their dick more."

"I'm surprised you didn't say that I would play with my dick more if I could find it since you think you're da man with all the jokes," Rico replied quickly, heading off any attempt by Trevor to crack another joke.

"I was about to Rico, but it's no fun when you anticipate my move." They both laughed again.

"It was Sharon. Yeah that was her name. I'm sure of it!"

"Yeah Rico, I got you."

BRUCE ENTERED THE apartment carrying a bulky, large screen television that seemed even bigger when hoisted by his smallish frame. Bruce's light brown face, replete with an assortment of small marks, scars and minor skin discolorations—the direct result of his battle clad lifestyle—showed no hint of strain. Although his face was weathered and worn from a great many violent conflicts, he was not an unattractive man. On the contrary, many women found him ruggedly handsome, and his raw masculinity attractive. In fact, it was common knowledge that Bruce had slept with more women than both Trevor and Rico combined. A little factoid that Bruce was quick to remind them of whenever one of them started bragging about their sexual prowess.

Bruce Eric Peterson was barely five feet nine and had a deceivingly slight build. What few knew until it was too late was that he was made from pure granite. The way a person would understand the constricting power of a python once fatefully locked in its smothering embrace. His body was taut with sinewy muscle and he was gifted with unlimited endurance and energy.

His forearms were Popeye-like and were connected to fists the size of small melons. His neck was solid and stretched thickly at its base; it easily could have belonged to a man twice his size and weight. None of this, however, was evident to the untrained eye because of his slight build. His clothes didn't stretch trying to contain bulging muscles; rather they hung unimpressively on his frame. But for those who saw him at the neighborhood pool or shirtless on a hot summer day, they knew how awe inspiring his physique was. Thoughts of Bruce Lee's ripped body in the movie *Enter the Dragon* came to mind.

As impressive as he was physically, his indomitable will and innate ability to find his opponent's weakness gave him an almost unfair advantage over most of his adversaries. He had a real yet almost superhuman ability to ignore pain which would break down an opponent's will over the course of a fight. He honed his fighting acumen early in life on the grassy fields across the street from the city's most notorious junior high school.

Bruce was sort of a mythical figure like a ghetto version of Hercules or Sampson. Trevor first heard only stories and rumors about his violent encounters and feats of strength. At the age of nine he took the chain off his bicycle and used it to beat to a bloody pulp one of the notorious Richfield brothers, who was four years his elder at the time. According to legend, Jeffrey Richfield had made the mistake of cursing at Bruce's grandmother, something that he would live to regret. He would carry around a four-inch scar from that bicycle chain impacting his forehead as a constant reminder of Bruce's uncontrollable rage towards those whom he thought slighted him.

Trevor and Rico met up with Bruce a few years later at Bishop Bentley and had a front row seat to all the carnage, watching him tear through some of the toughest, meanest kids in the tri-city area. Anyone who thought they could lay claim to his title as the king of Bishop Bentley Junior High School was subject to the most severe ass kicking they'd ever faced.

Bishop Bentley was located in a very affluent part of the city, surrounded by rolling grassy hills and beautiful Victorian style homes with well-manicured lawns. The aesthetic of school was like a postcard, but the outward beauty and sensibility belayed the violence that ran rampant though its tiled hallways and blackboard classrooms.

Bishop Bentley School had two major issues. The first was the majority of the teachers were racist while the rest were apathetic. The majority of students, who were black, felt disenfranchised. The other issue was the vice-principal, a six-foot-five 230-pound former Irish dockworker and Navy SEAL, had developed a well-earned reputation as a disciplinary educator. With the emphasis on disciplinary. Simply put, he took no shit and would dish out punishment to even the toughest kids, which often included a stiff backhand or his favorite finishing move: a vice-like hand clamp to the back of the neck.

The city's school board, in all its wisdom, decided to make Bishop Bentley the last stop for every troubled kid and malcontent in the city's network of junior high schools. If a student was suspended from a junior high on the South Side, once reinstated he would be transferred to Bishop Bentley. His last stop before permanent expulsion. Bishop quickly became a repository, a holding tank for some of the worst kids in the city. Most were already hardened criminals; others were just plain psychotic, all of whom would spend some time in prison. Those other junior highs were all but willing to open their floodgates and dumped the most incorrigible, despicable group of juvenile delinquents into the open arms of Bishop Bentley.

Bruce was the undisputed king of Bishop Bentley and had been since the sixth grade. Although he had several fights before, he officially got the title when he destroyed an eighth grader named Robert "Big House" Jackson. The fight lasted ten minutes, and for the first five Big House looked like the probable victor. He threw a lot of punches and even knocked Bruce to the ground a few times, but at the six minute mark of the fistfight he could barely lift his arms due to fatigue and exhaustion.

Bruce on the other hand was just warming up. He kicked him solidly in the chest, causing what little air he had left to quickly exit, dropping him flat to the ground with a thud. Bruce jumped on him and pummeled him with punches to all parts of his body for the next five minutes. The result was a broken nose, two fractured ribs, a bruised kidney. He was in the hospital for a week and soon after his release he moved to Baltimore to live with an uncle.

Bruce, Trevor, and Rico were just entering the seventh grade when the influx of incorrigibles from the other junior high schools started in earnest. Bruce seemed to welcome the challenge. He relished the opportunity to prove himself. He was cut from a different cloth. Each week he eagerly awaited to see who the next challenger would be to try to dethrone him and capture his mythical title. And there were plenty of challengers. Transfers arrived weekly like raw sewage through old rotting drainage pipes. To the students of Bishop Bentley, Bruce was known as "King B," but he preferred "The Duke," which was later shortened to just "Duke." He considered himself a John Wayne-like character: a gunslinger taking on all comers in the Wild West of those Saturday afternoon matinees.

"I knew it! You two are up here having fun, laughing and shit, while I'm busting my ass doing all the hard work!" Bruce barked while holding the nineteen-inch Sony television in his arms without the slightest hint of strain in his face. Bruce's voice was equally deceiving: high pitched with a slightly nasal overtone. Not the voice of a furious man of fisticuffs.

"Did you hear that Rico lost thirty pounds?" Trevor said sarcastically to Bruce.

"Big deal, he loses thirty pounds every time he takes a shit. He'll put it back on at his next visit to Zack's Diner. Let's grab that black leather sofa next," Bruce replied without changing his expression. Seconds later, their uncontrollable laughter resonated through the hallway.

TREVOR RETURNED TO his apartment after a quick trip to his parents' home in nearby Greenville, roughly a forty-five-minute trip, to find a note taped to his door:

Attention: Miss Stillwell: New Tenant—Apartment 3A

It has come to my attention that you have had a frequent male visitor to your apartment. While having male visitors is not prohibited, you cannot have another person share the apartment or move in without the expressed written approval of the property manager. The individual whom I am referring to seems to have keys to your apartment and has been seen in the building at all times of day and night. Please address this situation before further action is taken.

Arthur Baxter—Hillcrest Apartment Manager

A **DAY HAD PASSED** since Trevor found the note on his door. He wasn't in a rush to respond; after all he had paid three months' rent in advance and knew that the mix-up could be easily remedied. He wasn't concerned in the least. Besides, his mind was focused on the big day ahead. He was meeting with his soon-to-be employer, Mr. Marvin Moncrieff, the president and CEO of the largest asset acquisition and public relations firm in town at 9:00 a.m. sharp. Trevor relaxed on his new black leather couch and thumbed through Montcrieff Marketing Inc.'s latest annual report. The television played softly in the background and before long he drifted off to sleep.

There was a soft knock at his door. The first few knocks became a part of his dreamscape, but as they continued, he slowly awoke.

She was dressed in only a blue satin nightshirt. The remnants of tears were etched on her tawny face.

"Hi, remember me?" she said in a shaky voice.

"Hi...of course I do. Are...are you okay?" Trevor tried to gather himself and hoped that he did sound as surprised as he felt.

"I'm okay, I just want to stop by to—"

Before she could finish Trevor interrupted her. "Wait, please come inside; don't stand in the doorway."

He stepped to the side, opening the door completely. She walked in assuredly and without hesitating, which surprised Trevor even more than her unexpected visit. "Please have a seat. I'm kind of still unpacking, so ignore the mess."

She looked around the room and made an inquisitive facial expression, as if to say, what mess. She started to speak as he made his way to join her on the couch. "I just wanted to apologize for the way I behaved the other day. I had a lot on my mind. I wasn't being myself." She sat stiffly; her legs closed tightly, her hands uncomfortably placed on her lap.

"No need to apologize, really. I enjoyed your company. You know talking is really overrated anyway." She smiled at that. "I did really enjoy just being around you, even if you weren't having the best of days." Trevor was sincere and naturally knew what to say to make a girl feel good.

"That's a nice thing to say." Her topaz eyes welled with tears.

"I mean it. You strike me as the kind of woman a man would enjoy just spending time with no matter the circumstances." She smiled again as a singular tear broke the dam of her eyelids and streamed down her face.

"Are you okay? Can I do something to help?" Trevor responded instinctively to her tears by gently wiping them from her face with his thumb. His hand caressed her face momentarily.

"I'm just a little upset. Things just haven't been going well for me lately."

"Is it anything you want to talk about?" Trevor said as he felt the moistness of her tears on his fingertips.

"No, not really…I just wanted to let you know that I think you're really nice and I didn't mean to leave you with the wrong impression the other day."

"You didn't leave a bad impression at all. Everybody has bad stretches. I hardly know you but when there is something special about someone it doesn't take long to recognize it. I've been thinking about you since Sal's."

Staring into her water filled eyes, he again found himself wondering what could so deeply trouble such a beautiful woman. Then he noticed her slowly inching closer to him. At first, he thought it was his imagination, but she was slowly leaning towards him. She rested her head on his chest. Trevor instinctively wrapped his arms tenderly around her and held her firm and close. He wanted her to feel secure and protected.

She felt good to him. He instinctively smelled her hair then gently circled his chin on the top of her head. Trevor knew that a good barometer of a woman was how she felt in his arms and how she smelled. The smell of a woman's neck, or at her hairline, and of course, the vitally important kiss. He was convinced that he could feel her passion through their embrace and their chemistry was tied to smell. To Trevor there was nothing as intimate, as personal, or as telling as the kiss. The way she responded to his touch and the soothing smell of her skin caused Trevor's body to ache. It was as fresh as the light breeze that stirred a warm summer night. He found himself wishing their embrace would last for more than just a few fleeting moments.

She lifted her head and pursed her lips. He gently pressed his lips against hers, and then gently pulled away, but only momentarily. He pressed his lips against hers again and stayed there for a moment longer. The next time he pressed his lips against hers she opened her mouth just enough to let Trevor's tongue slip in and circle the contour of the moist lips. *Yeah,* Trevor thought to himself, *she can kiss.*

"Are you sure I can't do something to help you?" He softly kissed the top of her head.

"You could let me spend the night with you." Trevor was again surprised that evening. Very pleasantly surprised.

THE MEETINGS AT Montcrieff Marketing, Inc. the following morning started inauspiciously and were rather perfunctory, much as Trevor had expected. He briefly met the man who would be his direct report-to, the COO James Rhodes, a former marine who had a keen mind and a sharp tongue. Mr. Rhodes had a reputation for telling it like it was. He wasn't a person overly concerned with hurting people's feelings. They discussed his future duties and responsibilities as well as major projects he was expected to quickly get up to speed on. Trevor spent most of the early part of the morning meeting with people from the Personnel Department and completing form after form, answering question after question.

There was a series of questions on the employment form that caused Trevor to pause and do some self-reflecting: "Have you ever been convicted of a crime, check felony or misdemeanor, and detail?" He lifted the pen in the air and rubbed the back of it against his forehead. The answer to the question was a resounding no, but Trevor knew much of the credit for him being able to provide that answer rested squarely on the shoulders of his wayward friend "The Duke."

Trevor always wondered how Bruce had managed to get him out of so many tight situations but couldn't prevent his own trouble with the law, which would ultimately lead to a couple of stints behind bars. Bruce had been in and out of jail during most of the time Trevor was in high school and college. Never for very long though, mostly ninety-day to three-months stints at a time. But from the time they met in the corridors of Bishop Bentley Junior High, Bruce was constantly in and out of trouble with the law. He had been arrested for breaking and entering, possession of stolen goods, possession of a controlled substance, grand theft auto, and possession of a concealed weapon, but his main legal infraction, by far, was assault and battery, which littered multiple pages of his lengthy rap sheet. While Trevor was majoring in Sociology and Business Marketing at Mathias College, Bruce was accumulating credits in the field of Hard Knocks at Street Life University.

"Mr. Stillwell." The secretary seated behind the large glass desk was calling out his name. The woman was probably in her mid-forties but didn't look a day over thirty. She had engaging pear-shaped icy green eyes, a smooth creamy complexion, and full lips that appeared to be in constant anticipation of her lover's kiss. She wore a smart turquoise two-piece suit with a matching checkered scarf draped delicately around her neck. Her hair was stylishly layered in a twist of three braids just above her forehead. She placed a pair of small dark rimmed glasses on her face before speaking, which Trevor thought gave her a sexy schoolteacher kind of vibe. *Can I stay after school?* he thought to himself, and smiled.

"Yes," Trevor responded, snapping himself out of his schoolboy haze.

"Mr. Moncrieff would like to see you before you leave. He's in the conference room on the fifth floor." She smiled invitingly at Trevor and he returned it.

THE ROOM WAS spacious, encased by large windows spanning ceiling to floor and overlooking the West Side of the city. The room had an elegant and graceful feel but with very masculine colors and undertones. A large oak conference table laced with polished brass dominated the center of the room. It was reminiscent of King Arthur's round table, sturdy and intricately designed.

Mr. Marvin Moncrieff sat somewhat stoically at the head of the table. He was a handsome, meticulously manicured sixty-year-old black man. His thin brown face extended to a slightly receding hairline and a pronounced widow's peak. He wore a perfectly tailored European cut double-breasted suit, light gray with black pinstripes. The cuffs of his shirt were embroidered with his initials and adorned with eighteen-karat gold cufflinks that had the insignia of the college where he earned a master's in finance. Trevor knew that the man seated before him had attended one of the most prestigious business schools in the world.

"Come in Trevor. Have a seat right here." Mr. Moncrieff motioned Trevor toward the seat on his right. He was the personification of class; his voice was smooth and had a melodic tone. He was the epitome of a dignified and highly successful black man. This was the second time that Trevor had sat down with him. And on both occasions, he sensed an avuncular connection with Mr. Moncrieff.

As Trevor pulled out one of the large throne-like chairs to sit, Mr. Moncrieff stood and walked over to the windows. "Did you know that I started this business in a broken-down storefront on Sassafras Avenue?"

"Yes, sir. I know that you started your business in 1962 at age twenty-five. In your first year through sheer will and determination you landed the *Jet Magazine* account and posted revenues in excess of fifty thousand dollars. Over the next ten years your client base grew to include *Ebony*, *Life*, and *Sports Illustrated*. You grew from a one-man operation to a staff of twenty-five, including your brother Wilbur who heads your West Coast operations. In 1977 you branched into television and radio communications and started working with the big boys—Ford, Time Publications, and General Mills, and what was at that time a fledgling Japanese electronics manufacturer, Sony. Today you run the most successful minority-owned public relations/media company whose corporate creativity is the envy of the industry."

"I'm impressed, Mr. Stillwell," Mr. Moncrieff said convincingly, still gazing out the window.

"That's just doing my research Mr. Moncrieff. My due diligence. If you want me to really impress you, just wait until I start actually working for you."

"A confident and intelligent young black man. You remind me of myself at your age. Of course, I didn't graduate top of my class with a fancy degree from a fancy private college. I only had half a degree from city junior college, but then I parlayed that into a masters from Grayson's College. You work with what you have. You've done that too: smart, aggressive, and confident. Those are important characteristics Mr. Stillwell."

"That's a great compliment Mr. Moncrieff. Thank you so much and please call me Trevor."

"Trevor?" Mr. Moncrieff inquisitively replied.

Trevor knew exactly why Mr. Moncrieff had that particular look of surprise on his face.

"That's fine with me. Trevor it is then."

He continued, "I asked you up here because I've been thinking about something ever since we first met. What was that, several weeks ago?" Trevor nodded in agreement.

There was an awkward silence, but Trevor patiently waited for him to continue. "Behind your intelligent, articulate, and well-mannered demeanor I sense something else…something that's very familiar to me. I don't know your background beyond what appears on your résumé but I sense that you've had to overcome some tremendous obstacles to get to this point in your life?"

Before Trevor could respond Mr. Moncrieff stood up, walked over, and stared out the window. The window cast such a distinct reflection of him that Trevor though was looking at a mirror. "You've had to navigate some pretty tricky waters to make it this far, haven't you Trevor?"

Trevor thought about downplaying his background and telling Mr. Moncrieff that his life wasn't really all that challenging even though it was, but he felt compelled to speak honestly to this pillar of a man standing before him.

"I guess you could say that. Growing up in the housing projects and spending most of your free time hanging at The Mose aren't exactly harbingers of success or indications of life on easy street. Is it that obvious?"

"Not at all, in fact quite the contrary, Trevor. It just takes one to know one. Trevor, the lessons you've learned by overcoming the pitfalls of the streets will prove more valuable than anything you've learned in college. Trust me on that one. Finding success in corporate America as a black man is extremely difficult, and without the street sense and survival instincts I learned growing up in Watts during the '50s, I wouldn't be where I'm at today. I've drawn on my street instincts more than a few times while fighting battles in the boardroom. I've found them very useful, whether it was to persuade, cajole, or intimidate. I consider those instincts an asset.

"Just be careful; just because you've overcome the pitfalls of the streets doesn't mean the street can't still come back to bite you in the ass if you're not being vigilant. It may be an old debt looking to settle or an old friend looking for your help. Street savvy can be a double-edged sword, Trevor. Don't be too confident when you're out there, it's a game you can never truly master." He turned and silently gazed out the window again. Seemingly lost in his own thoughts.

Mr. Moncrieff's words weighted heavily on Trevor's mind during the silence that ensued. He was surprised this man of business and industry thought that street smarts were so valuable a commodity. The relationship between the streets and the boardroom didn't quite connect for Trevor but he found himself trusting the words of the sharply dressed black man standing in front of him. But he also sensed that this impenetrable black man was battling his own demons. Trevor could feel that something was weighing heavily on his mind.

Mr. Moncrieff slowly walked over to Trevor and pulled out a chair so close to Trevor that their knees almost touched. "You see Trevor, every time I have an opening on one of my marketing project teams, I get a shitload of résumés. For the new project coordinator's position we hired you to fill, we received over a thousand résumés on the first day. Now granted, you made it through the first few rounds of interviews based solely on your academic record and interview skills, but I chose you because I sense in you that 'X factor' that the other ten finalists didn't possess."

Trevor listened intently, transfixed by the words he heard.

"I sensed when we first met that you were a perceptive young man, a good judge of character like myself. You know people and their motivations, see through the bullshit that most people come at you with, to get people to do what you want them to do. What I don't know is, do you have the stick-to-itiveness to persevere through challenging situations? Those are all invaluable skills Trevor and that's what this company needs as we embark on a time of significant growth. Because this business is all about understanding, communicating with, and persuading people."

Trevor listened intently, feeling somewhat like an open book. It was obvious to him that Mr. Moncrieff was also a very astute judge of character. He was a man who understood the value of the lessons of the streets—what to take from them and what to leave behind. Something Trevor still struggled with.

Mr. Moncrieff stood and walked toward the window and by doing so, changed the direction of their conversation. "I understand that Ms. Stillson was able to find you a suitable apartment."

"Yes, sir. I have a nice spacious place at the Hillcrest Apartments over on Sassafras. Your old stomping grounds."

"At the Hillcrest, huh?" Mr. Moncrieff stroked his chin with the palm of his hand and Trevor couldn't help but notice his well-manicured hands and matching diamond studded wedding band and bracelet. "I almost bought that place a few years ago but the owner backed out of the deal at the last minute. I really wanted that place. It's a nice piece of investment property and I don't own anything in that part of town anymore. My wife loves to shop over there but I'm partial to the Cambodian cuisine myself."

Trevor's curiosity was piqued by Mr. Moncrieff's comments about the Hillcrest and he was tempted to ask a question, but decided against it.

Mr. Moncrieff walked the length of the room with his arms folded before speaking again. "You start here in a few weeks?"

"Next Monday sir."

"Would you be interested in working on a special project that I've been thinking about? It will require a lot of creative thought and you would be reporting directly to me."

"I am your man, sir!"

HERE WAS A thunderous knock at the front door of his apartment. Trevor had just gotten into the shower when he heard it. He had told Bruce nine o'clock and it was only 8:20 p.m., but Trevor knew Bruce liked to be early. "Hold your horses!" he yelled as he wrapped a towel around his waist. He considered putting his bathrobe on before answering the door, but then came another monstrous bang.

He angrily opened the door ready to get in Bruce's ass for trying to break his door down only find two men standing in the hallway: one a mountain of man dressed in a tight-fitting black T-shirt and jeans, the other a more diminutive man, dressed in a baggy red Adidas sweat suit. Both men were complete strangers to Trevor. His emotions did a complete one hundred and eighty degree turn from anger to surprise and then apprehension.

Who are these two? he thought to himself. A sneaking feeling of dread was creeping up his spine. He was about to slam the door shut, lock it, and race to his bedroom to retrieve the only weapon he had in his new apartment—a nine-iron golf club—when he noticed that the bigger of the two was trying to conceal something behind his back. This distracted Trevor just enough to cause him not to act on his flight feeling, something he would soon regret.

"Do you live here?" the smaller man asked in an aggressive tone.

"What business is it of yours?" Trevor replied in a burst of anger laced with fear.

He knew that something was about to go down and he wished that he listened to his flight instincts. Trevor rocked slightly back but before he could ready himself the large man charged him and tackled him into the apartment. The other man picked up the baseball bat that the big man had behind his back and dropped while charging Trevor, and closed the door behind him.

Trevor was pinned on the floor under the weight of the large man. He struggled to free himself but couldn't. "Let him up Roscoe," said the smaller man.

Roscoe stood up and stepped backward, allowing Trevor to retrieve his towel, which had fallen on the floor, and regain his feet. "What the fuck's going on?!" Trevor barked as he adjusted the towel around his waist.

The smaller man displayed the bat and in a show of strength pounded the head of the bat into the palm of his left hand. "Shut up and sit the hell down! We'll do all the axin' around here, chump."

Trevor moved cautiously toward the couch, never taking his eyes off either of the intruders.

"Now where's...huh...what's her name again?" He looked at the big man for an answer but only received a shoulder shrug from Roscoe. Reaching into his pocket he removed a crumpled piece of paper. Reading from the paper he spoke. "Oh, yeah, right...Kim. Where's Kim Stillwell—where she at?" Trevor knew the answer to that simple question but wasn't going to say anything.

Several seconds passed. "Not givin' up any answers huh? Well Roscoe here will be more than happy to put his foot up your ass if you wanna play dumb." The small man tossed the bat to Roscoe.

"What do you guys want? I don't even know who you guys

are!" Trevor's anxiety level was heading for the uncharted heights. He could feel his blood pumping through his veins and his breathing started to become more labored. He tried his best to quell the anxiety and calm himself.

"What'd I tell you about the questions? We axin', not you. You live here with Kim?" The smaller man started to circle around the left side of the couch. Trevor watched his movements intently; he noticed that the small man's fists were now tightly clenched. But taking his eye off Roscoe was his mistake. The handle of the bat crashed into Trevor's temple, forcefully knocking him into the arm of the couch.

Trevor saw a blast of red and then felt excruciating pain emanating from his forehead. Dazed and bleeding, another knock came at the door. Trevor's assailants looked confusedly at each other before a second knock resonated through the living room. The small man motioned for Trevor to keep quiet. After a third much louder knock the small man spoke to Trevor in a low tone. "Answer that door punk and get rid of whoever it is or they gonna catch an ass-whopping too."

Trevor stood uneasily and staggered slightly as he walked toward the door, but regained his normal gait within a few steps. He instinctively wiped his forehead, stemming the flow of the blood trickling down from the wound. He drew a short breath before opening the door. Opening it only slightly, he tried to focus his eyes on the figure standing in the hallway.

"What's up Trev? You ready or what man?" Bruce looked Trevor in the eye but was seemingly unaware of the blood coming from the three-inch cut on his forehead, the quickly developing knot, or the distress etched on Trevor's face.

Trevor's voice cracked slightly. "No, man...I...I can't. I can't go now. I'll have to check you out later." A bolt of blood streamed down Trevor's forehead before he closed the door. He pretended to turn the lock on the door and slowly walked back to the couch.

"Good work punk ass nigga! Saved your friend some serious problems. Now sit your fucking ass back on dat couch so we can finish our bidness." The smaller man moved from behind the couch to the window. He peeked from behind the curtain to see who was exiting the building.

Trevor sat and thought of the irony of his predicament. Last night he was making love to a beautiful girl on the same couch that he was now bleeding on. He knew that the other shoe would surely drop; he just didn't expect it to happen so soon. He knew after a beautiful woman entered his life trouble followed. He was sure there was some relationship between that girl last night and these two fools fucking with him. It was no coincidence. It wasn't the first time and surely wouldn't be the last. It had been Trevor's experience that beautiful women were synonymous with trouble, a harbinger of sorts. If it wasn't this kind of trouble, then it was heartbreak or some other negative life-altering occurrence. He wondered how many times he would have to learn the same lesson.

A force swiftly entered the room like a rush of strong wind. Roscoe turned and was assaulted by a barrage of heavy punches that dropped him to a knee. The last punch was a hard right cross that Bruce threw from above his head and landed with a resounding thud and rocked Roscoe's jaw from east to west. Roscoe was laid out on the floor in less than five seconds.

Bruce picked up the bat and charged the other man, who initially took a boxing stance but then seemed to realize that the large baseball bat gave his adversary an insurmountable advantage. He quickly darted around the other side of the couch and headed for the door. As he stepped into the hallway he was struck squarely in the back by the flying wooden projectile. **THUD!** The sound of the bat making contact with his upper back and shoulder region was loud and resonated down the hallway. The sheer force with which Bruce hurled the baseball bat was astounding and when it made contact with the man he was instantly felled. Before he even knew what hit him Bruce was on him, pummeling him with powerfully punches to the head and chest, including a hard elbow to the temple. Unconsciousness came mercifully for the man in the red Adidas sweat suit.

Bruce rose calmly and with a deep exhale spoke. "You okay Trev?"

Roscoe moaned and attempted to roll over on his back. Trevor stepped quickly from the couch and smashed the heel of his foot into the side of Roscoe's head several times until all movement stopped.

Trevor and Bruce stood silently over the motionless bodies. Bruce moved to the doorway and stood there; Trevor stood in the apartment. "Damn Trev, what the fuck's going on, you owe someone money or messing someone's girl?"

Trevor reached down and rubbed the sole of his foot. "I don't know what's going now and I don't owe anyone money and can't say if it's about a woman!"

"Because these cats seem like strong-arm types. You know, leg breakers for a bookie. Thugs for hire." Bruce looked down at the bodies of his defeated foes.

"Duke, I don't owe anyone anything and I don't know who these guys are, but I do know that I better find out what's going on and fast." Trevor called Bruce by his old moniker, a fact that didn't go unnoticed by Bruce.

"You haven't called me that in a while, Trev. I missed you calling me that man." Bruce stepped over the body of the small man and reentered the apartment.

"I guess watching you waste these two assholes brought back some old memories," Trevor replied.

"I know what you mean, being on probation these past few years I've hadda try my best to avoid getting into any beefs… but this shit felt good…real fuckin' good." Bruce balled up his large fist and started shadowboxing with a ferocity that few men possessed.

"That's good for you but this shit doesn't feel so good to me!" Trevor gently swiped his forehead with his hand, wincing slightly when he touched the gash. "What do we do with these fools now?"

"First thing first, put on some damn clothes and then we'll drag dese two tough guys down the hall. We'll leave em' in the rear stairwell."

"What happens when they wake up?"

"They'll go home and lick their wounds and ask their boss what to do next," Bruce said confidently.

"You really think they're working for someone?"

"For sure, Trev."

"Do you think they'll be back tonight?"

"Tonight? Not likely. They know you'll be prepared, have reinforcements and shit, but it all depends on what their boss tell em." The sureness of Bruce's words was not lost on Trevor.

"Then I guess I've got some work to do," Trevor replied.

"What?" Bruce said, bewildered and confused.

Trevor was surprised by his tone and tried to explain. "Duke, I've got to figure out why these guys are after me, I've got to be ready to go to battle if need be. You know how this shit works."

"Trev, that's not what I mean. What's up with this 'I' shit man; this is a 'We' thing now. We're in this thing together! Now nobody fucks with my main man Trevor with impunity."

Trevor smiled slightly. "Impunity, huh?"

"Yeah, well I guess your educated ass is rubbing off on me."

T**HE SKY BLUE** 1972 Cadillac Coupe Deville pulled sharply away from the curb and sped down Sassafras Avenue. The quiet hum of the engine was barely audible against the backdrop of the bustling streets of the city at night.

"Stop at the hardware store on Royal. I need to get a new lock for my apartment," Trevor said to Bruce.

"Trev, don't ya hafta get permission from someone before you go changin' locks and shit? You wouldn't wanna break the law." Bruce smiled sheepishly. "You know that you're not cut out to do no jail time now, college boy."

"Relax man, I'll talk to the property manager tomorrow and I'll change them back if I have to..." Trevor's face tightened. "I'm not sure but I could've sworn I heard the lock jiggle before I opened the door to find those two thugs standing there."

"You think they were trying to jimmy your lock?" Bruce questioned.

"I don't know? Sounded more like a key being inserted."

"What, are you saying that they had a key to your place?" Bruce gave Trevor a perplexed look.

"Never mind. It was probably my imagination but I'll feel better if I change the lock anyway."

The music playing quietly in the car started to drag. Bruce gently tapped the stereo component in the dashboard and it returned to normal. "See, I got a gentle touch too, Trev." Bruce gently patted the dashboard.

Trevor slumped deeper into his seat. "Yeah, I hear you, but keep your eyes on the road." A minute later the music started to drag again.

"Damnm it!" exclaimed Bruce, this time hitting the console with his fist.

Trevor thought to tell him to be careful—he might damage the dashboard—but he knew his words would fall on deaf ears. Hitting stuff was Bruce's way of handling every problem.

After a quick stop at Fred's Hardware and Convenience Store on Royal Avenue, they continued driving toward the West Side.

"Where are we going anyway?" Trevor asked casually. Not really caring, just happy to be extricated from the situation at his apartment and to be driving around and clearing his head.

"Relax Trev, I should be taking your ass to the hospital to get some stitches."

In addition to the lock, Trevor also bought a large butterfly bandage which, once awkwardly positioned on his forehead, stemmed the last trickles of blood leaking from his wound.

Bruce looked at Trevor and motioned him to wipe some blood that had dripped down his face and gathered at the corner of his mouth.

"Damn Trev, you couldn't taste that?"

"Taste what?"

"All that blood on the corner of your mouth."

"Damn, I know this isn't going to be totally healed by the time I start my new job. Ain't that a bitch!" Trevor exclaimed.

"See Trev, you're thinking too much so that means it is my job to get you mind off all this shit for a minute, so that's where we're going. TO GET YOUR MIND OFF!" Bruce shouted excitedly out the car window.

"What's that supposed to mean to me and how the hell do

you expect me to relax my mind when you're doing seventy-five down a city street?"

"Man, you know I'm a driving fool." At the approaching intersection the light changed to yellow. Bruce pressed hard on the accelerator. The big car seemed to pounce forward like a cat on an unsuspecting mouse. It raced through the crosswalk as the light turned to red.

Trevor's body tensed and then relaxed all in one motion. "The emphasis on FOOL!"

"I s'pose I was a fool when I arrived at your apartment in the nick of time too, right?"

Trevor relaxed and leaned back into the comfort of the soft tan leather bucket seat, closed his eyes and tried to forget the events of the past few hours. No words were exchanged until the car turned into a dirty, dust-strewn parking lot.

"Where are we?" Trevor asked, looking out the passenger side window.

"We're at the Palace. The Secret Palace to be exact," Bruce responded with his usual wry smile.

"A strip club?" Trevor's voice was laced with disappointment.

"A Gentlemen's Club," Bruce replied proudly.

"Bruce you know I am not in the mood to go to a titty bar tonight."

"What? You not into pussy?" Bruce looked at Trevor with an exaggerated expression.

"Stop messing around man, you know what I mean. I'm not dressed for this right now and I got a damn bandage on my head."

"Like you ain't pulled women looking worse. Don't worry, this place is causal; we'll just grab one drink, I promise."

Trevor knew that he would lose any ensuing argument and decided to acquiesce and just go with the flow, but he wasn't happy about it in the slightest.

Bruce circled the parking lot looking for a parking space. With an impatient hard turn of the wheel, the car zoomed toward the entrance of the club. "Fuck this! I'm going to park right up front next to that Bentley."

Trevor recognized the cream-colored car immediately.

"Now that's a car!" Bruce exclaimed. "But why would anyone have it in such a bitch ass color. If that shit were mine it be jet black," Bruce said excitedly.

There were not many things that excited him more than cars. They were one of his three tiered passions: pussy, cars, and fighting. Depending on the circumstances their order of importance would change. At present that Bentley was edging out pussy by a yard.

They stepped out of the car. "Damn! Look how clean that shit is, Trev." Bruce was consumed with admiration for the car.

Trevor always thought that Bruce's penchant for stealing cars when he was a teenager was based more on his fascination with the cars themselves than the tidy financial gain he acquired by selling them to chop shops after a weekend of joyriding.

His desire to possess luxury cars rivaled the passion most men have for beautiful seductive women.

Trevor studied the license plate of the Bentley as they walked past. M A T E O 1. "If this was five years ago, I'd be tempted to make that car mine for the weekend," Bruce said assuredly.

Trevor disapprovingly shook his head. "Relax Trev, I'm on the straight and narrow now, like you man." After a few more steps, Bruce stopped and shook his foot to remove the dirt that had gathered from the unpaved parking lot. "But on the real Trev, if I don't find a decent paying job soon, I'm gonna hafta do what I gotta do to get paid. I just want you to know that."

Trevor knew that Bruce was running out of patience with trying to walk the straight and narrow.

The Palace was located in the smallest of a group of interconnected single story abandoned buildings. Although it was located only a few blocks from the thriving downtown business district, if you didn't know exactly where you were going you would never find it. Railroad tracks and blighted storefronts obscured it from street view. If you were lucky enough to find your way into the patch of dirt used for parking, a small illuminated sign near the back of the building was its only calling card.

Once through the set of large wooden oval-shaped doors, reminiscent of a castle's gateway, Trevor and Bruce walked down a long dimly lit hallway. Two women were positioned at the end of the walkway. One stood behind a podium, the other was seated in front of the small room used as a coat check.

"Welcome to the palace," they said almost in unison.

They were both very attractive women, but the one at the coat check immediately caught Trevor's eye. While Bruce paid the cover charge to the woman at the podium, Trevor couldn't stop watching the girl at the coat check as she pulled back her long-braided hair into a ponytail. She wore a light blue eye shadow and silvery lip gloss that embraced her long thin lips. Her finely outlined eyebrows accented the soft features of her deep beige complexioned face.

She seemed unaware of Trevor's amorous stare. "Enjoy yourselves gentlemen," said the Afro-Asiatic looking woman at the podium.

"Huh…yeah…thanks…" Trevor stammered out the words while still transfixed on the girl seated at the coat check.

"Trev, you are staring like crazy man. C'mon, can we go in? There's more inside you know," Bruce said with more than a hint of sarcasm.

"More what?"

"Damn Trev, that knock on your head must've loosened a screw or two because you're kind of slow on the uptake tonight."

They entered a large room that had more length than width to it. The club was designed to resemble an Arabian palace—replete with rich red carpets, chairs that mimicked miniature thrones, and large couch-like pillows arranged in circular patterns along the far walls. Intricate Muslim motifs covered the walls and ceiling. Individual folding partitions provided both intimacy and atmosphere and separated each set of tables in the lower corner of the room. However, only half the room was complete; the far end of the room was unfinished, with bare, unpainted drywall and exposed light fixtures.

There were two horseshoe-shaped bars located at either end of the room. Trevor and Bruce took seats at the bar nearest the entrance. "This place is nice, right?" Bruce asked as he motioned to one of the bartenders.

"Yeah, man, I like the vibe in here," Trevor said in a relaxed tone.

"Look around Trev, notice anything different 'bout this place?"

Trevor casually scanned the room. "Not really. You mean other than the 'Ali Baba and the Forty Thieves' décor?"

"What can I get you gentlemen?" the lovely bartender asked softly with an inviting smile.

Bruce turned to the bar and placed the order. "Two double shots of Remy and a Coke chaser."

Trevor continued to scan the room. Bruce laughed. "Man, you're not as observant as I thought you were, Trev. Haven't you noticed that everyone working here is a badass piece of ass? Never mind the dancers, look at the waitresses, bartenders, the two at the door."

Trevor quickly scanned the club again and Bruce was right. Not only was the club entirely staffed by women, they all were extremely attractive.

"I think the guy running this joint has an office behind that staging area in the back of the club. I've seen him go through that door near those big mirrors with encrusted gold frames."

Trevor had noticed that there were mirrors strategically

located throughout the club. Bruce pointed to a door directly under the largest of the mirrored windows.

"How many times have you been here?" Trevor asked.

"I've been coming here for about a month or so now and I've never seen anything other than fine ass females working here. I swear." Bruce spoke with the conviction of a religious zealot.

"It's a creative way of staffing a club, I'll give them that much. Who wouldn't want to come to a club that has nothing but beautiful women serving you?"

"That's for sure, but every time I'm up in this joint it's practically empty. That's why I keep coming back, the more pussy for me." Bruce lifted his shot glass and motioned for another before his empty glass hit the top of the bar.

Trevor spotted her as he turned to reach for his drink still resting on the bar. She wore a platinum wig with a long curl in the front that obscured her face slightly, but he was sure it was her. She was dancing seductively between the outstretched legs of a silver-haired white man wearing a smart blue pin-striped business suit. Before Trevor could get a better view of her, she took the man by his hand and led him through a door by the unfinished end of the club.

Trevor reached out and tugged on Bruce's shoulder. "Bruce, I know that girl."

"What girl?"

"You can't see her now; she went through that door over there." Trevor tried to inconspicuously point to the door.

"Hope he has enough money."

"Why?"

"Behind that door you can get a private lap dance or more, depending on how deep your pocket is."

"How do you know that?" Trevor asked in a surprised state.

Bruce didn't answer. He just gave Trevor a dumbfounded look as if to say, how do you think I know?

Trevor's mind was racing. He felt a slight pounding

coming from under his bandage. "How do you know that girl anyway?" Bruce inquired as he motioned to Trev that his head was bleeding again.

Trevor reached for a napkin and dabbed at his forehead. He looked at the crimson in the napkin and it reminded him of red paint on a clean canvas. "I don't really know her. I just remember seeing her the morning I moved into my apartment. I was looking out the window and she was walking down the street wearing a colorful sexy summer dress."

"So, you got a stripper living in your neighborhood. Big deal. Ain't like we ain't been there, done that. Remember that girl Nancy? She had the best pussy for sale 'round the hood..."

"...C'mon Bruce, let's not go there okay. I know all about your exploits with Nasty Nancy. No need to go there again. Besides not only does that girl live in my neighborhood, I think she lives in my building," Trevor said incredulously.

"Wait a minute!" Bruce turned his attention to Trevor. "That's kinda strange."

"What's strange?"

"Well me and Rico came here the night we helped you move in and he tried to tell me that two girls working here were the same two he saw earlier at your building."

"What?" Trevor nearly jumped out of his seat.

"That's some crazy ass coincidence, right?"

"Bruce, that's definitely no coincidence." Trevor swallowed the shot and slammed the glass on the bar.

Twenty minutes later they were back in Bruce's car driving back to the Hillcrest.

"Trevor I don't get it, so what if some of the girls from the club live at your place. What's that gotta do with the two dudes we tangled with earlier? I ain't never seen them at the club. There's no connection that I can see."

"Bruce, trust me, it's all connected. The club, the girls, and those dudes."

"Trev, you need to relax when I drop you off at your crib. You should go knock on that little chippy's door and get you some more of that ass tonight. Things will be clearer in the morning."

"Bruce, it's not like that, man." Trevor tried to knock holes in Bruce's assertion but knew if he was perfectly honest with himself there was some truth to his words. Trevor had been thinking about Tori all day.

"Trev, on the real man, the lock thing is cool and all that but I gotta little sumthin' sumthin' for you just in case." Bruce reached into the backseat of the car, under the passenger seat, and removed an object wrapped in a paper bag.

Trevor immediately knew what he was reaching for. "Damn Bruce, what are you doing carrying a piece in your car man? You're on probation man! What would happen if we got stopped for speeding or something? Neither one of us can afford that."

"Trev, you know I'd take the fall, if it came down to that. Nothing would happen to you."

"That's not the point, Bruce. What would happen to you?"

"I'd be calling you for bail," he replied with a halfhearted smile.

"Bail? You mean jail."

"Trev, you should know by now that we all take chances by just getting out of bed in the morning. It's just a matter of degrees, and trust me, if you don't take this piece you be taking a huge chance tonight with those clowns on your case."

"Is it hot?" Trevor said, already knowing the answer.

"Now Trev, you know that I can't go in a gun shop and buy a piece with my record. So yeah, of course it's stolen, but I've had it since the day it was boosted from some little gun shop near Brookdale, so it's never been used in a crime. Besides, it's virtually untraceable. I had my boy wipe it clean: no serial number, no nothing."

Bruce handed the package to Trevor. "I'll be giving this thing back to you tomorrow," Trevor replied, disappointed that he found himself in a position where he needed to carry a gun, yet again.

Trevor unwrapped the gun, turned the Beretta M9 from handle to barrel in his hand. He dropped the clip and closely examined it. "Damn, this is a sweet piece and double action too."

"Be careful with that Trevor, that's my baby. You'd blow a nigga to smithereens with that M9."

"Smithereens!" Trevor could hardly believe that Bruce had said that word.

"Who are you supposed to be, Quick Draw McGraw?"

Bruce started laughing hysterically. He laughed so hard and for so long that tears started rolling down his face. After about five minutes, Bruce was able to regain his composure. "Trev, what was Quick Draw's sidekick's name?"

"Baba Looey."

"That's right. Baba fuckin' Looey." Bruce started laughing again but couldn't quite muster the same enthusiasm. He was all laughed out.

Trevor discarded the paper in the backseat and tucked the small pistol in the small of his back, under his shirt, and exited the car. He thought of the conversation he had with Mr. Moncrieff about the streets coming back to bite you. This was surely what he was referring to.

"You still remember how to handle that thing, right?" Bruce asked inquisitively. Trevor closed the car door and knelt down beside the passenger door and just stared at Bruce. "Well, I guess it's like riding a bike?"

"Yeah, man, something like that," Trevor said in a low rumbled tone.

"Trev, you know I'm here for you man. We haven't always agreed on things, but I always got your back, Trev."

"Yeah, I know, and I appreciate that, man."

"I'll wait to hear from you, so don't get lost in that pussy. Remember it's on you to make sense of this whole thing. You are the former Mr. Fixit, the smart-ass college boy soon to be big shot businessman."

Bruce firmly grasped the steering wheel and shifted the gear into drive.

"I'm on it, man," Trevor replied.

"Au'ight then, I'll check you later. Oh, and tell that chippy I said hi." Bruce sped away with a screeching hard turn of the steering wheel. Trevor stood there and watched the Cadillac disappear into the blur of car headlights.

TREVOR HESITATED FOR a moment at the door before knocking. Sure, they had been together sexually, but he really didn't know much else about her, he thought to himself. Passion and lustful desire piloted that evening, so few words were exchanged. In the morning she was gone before he awoke. This time Trevor did remember to get her name and apartment number but very little else. A series of questions ran through his mind all at once. She never invited him to come by. Why? Did she consider their encounter a one-time tryst? Maybe she had a man? She might live with her man. Maybe she was married.

He looked at his watch, which read 12:30 a.m., and he considered walking away. His head was throbbing, but he really wanted to talk to her about what he saw at the club. He was hoping she could provide some of the missing pieces of information he was looking for.

"Who is it?" she asked from behind the door in a barely audible voice.

"It's Trevor," he replied, trying to mask the uncomfortable nature of this late-night intrusion.

Tori had been asleep; it was obvious to him the moment he looked into her heavy-lidded eyes. The light from the hallway cut across her face and disappeared into the darkness behind her. Peering through the slightly ajar door, she squinted as the bright light met her sleepy topaz eyes.

"Trevor, what's going on…is everything okay?" she said hesitantly. As her eyes adjusted to the light, she noticed the blood-soaked bandage on his forehead. "Trevor, what happened to your head?"

"It's okay, I'm fine but I need to talk to you. Can I come in?"

She hesitated again and looked back into her apartment. "If you have company, we can talk later," Trevor said, trying to hide his disappointment.

"No…don't be silly, I don't have company," she said reassuringly. "It's just that my apartment's a—"

"Listen, I really need to talk to you tonight. Please! I know it's late, but I need you." *That wasn't what I meant to say… or was it,* he thought. He looked away, not sure of his own emotions—betrayed by his own words. His words reflected his strong desire for her. *Bruce was right.*

She smiled and opened the door completely. He walked in from the illuminated hallway into complete darkness. Once she closed the door behind him, he was consumed by the shadows like a cloud before an oncoming storm. As his eyes started to adjust, he could make out the shadowy outlines of a crowded and disorganized room.

She took him by the arm and pulled him close to her. He placed the bag with the new lock and key on the box closest to him. "What's in the bag?" she asked as she opened her robe, baring her naked breast against his stomach.

"Nothing that can't wait," Trevor said as he deeply exhaled. He could feel her nipples stiffen as she circled them against his shirt. He passionately kissed her, tracing the contour of her lips with his tongue. He gently found the base of her neck and traced his tongue along her shoulder, up her neck until he reached the center of her ear. He slid the robe off her shoulders and dropped to a knee. He slipped his right hand around his back and removed the pistol, sliding the safety on and placing it on a small table without skipping a beat. He cupped her breast with his mouth; he slowly guided his tongue around her erect nipple until she moaned with pleasure.

He slowly lowered her to the floor and continued to caress her breasts with his tongue. He worked his way down, meticulously and passionately, stopping every few inches to embrace the softness of her skin until he was squarely positioned between her parted legs. He skillfully probed the contour of her opening with his tongue. He let her wetness soak his lips like a rain-drenched leaf. The taste and smell of her only ignited his passion to greater heights. He widened his tongue's path and licked her fully, entering her at regular intervals, to her escalating delight. She lifted her legs and placed them on his shoulders. She firmly placed her hands around his head, running her fingers through his hair.

After several intense minutes of orally pleasing her, he slowly pulled himself along her body until they were face-to-face. Lying on top of her with his body fully enveloping hers, he whispered to her, "Do you want to feel me inside you Tori?"

A loud moan was her only response. He moved his body in a circular motion in response to her moans. He could feel her legs start to quiver.

"Tell me? Tell me that you want to feel me inside you... deep inside you."

"Please," she said in an unsteady voice separated by heavy breaths.

As he entered her, her body twitched in ecstasy and she climaxed. Her body momentarily became limp and Trevor remained still, responding to the call of her body.

At the end of a long and forceful exhale she whispered to him, "You're not going to stop now, are you?" They both smiled in the darkness.

THEY SHOWERED TOGETHER and as the water cascaded off their intertwined bodies, they kissed passionately. With his hand firmly on her waist he slowly turned her and massaged her lower back. She instinctively bent forward slightly and reached around to grasp him firmly. She squeezed him tightly while rubbing him in a circular motion on the round soft cheeks of her buttock. She held him firmly as he expanded in her hand. Being in control of him excited her. She started stroking him more intensely. Trevor breathed heavily. She guided him down her center, until she reached her moistened lips. She released her grip, firmly planted the palms of her hand against the tiled shower wall, and forcefully pushed back with his every thrust until her legs again quivered in ecstasy.

The soft white cotton sheets of her bed were cool and comforting. The ceiling fan turned slowly and methodically, providing only a whisper of a breeze.

Over the next few hours Trevor found out much about the girl named Tori Anne White. She moved to town a year ago to attend a local private college, but when her scholarship was unexpectedly reduced, she had to take a job and charge her status to part-time student. She found temporary work clerking at a prestigious downtown law firm and planned on going back to school full-time in the fall. Now she was unemployed and for all intents and purposes, being evicted. She had no choice but to move back with her parents in Atlanta. Trevor comforted her while trying to piece together the puzzle that was developing before him.

She gathered some items from a box in a corner of the bedroom: antibiotic cream, a large Band-Aid and some hydrogen peroxide. She sat on the edge of the bed and had Trevor lay back and place the back of his head in her lap.

"Is this going to hurt?" Trevor asked jokingly.

"Not as much as when it happened, I'm sure. Now stop moving your head," she said as she steadied his head with her free hand.

As she swiped at the cut with a cloth drenched in peroxide, Trevor basked in the comforting touch. "Tori, do you know any of the other women in the building?" he asked.

"No, Sherry told me to stay to myself because most of the other women were jealous and petty."

Trevor smiled to himself. It always amazed him how distrustful women were of one another for no apparent reason. How easily they disparaged one another for superficial reasons. How vindictive and distrustful they were of one another, particularly when a man was involved.

His aunt Camilla was a perfect example. She was a magnificent and beautiful woman, with a broad empowering smile and a creamy beige complexion. Her boyfriend was caught cheating on her numerous times but every time she would tell Trevor's mother about how this bitch or that bitch is trifling and how bitches are always after someone else's man. When truth be told it was her man who was a no-good cheating bastard. He was an all-out dog and the majority of those other women were as much victims as she was. But she didn't see that way because her natural instincts clouded her thinking. Those instincts are so embedded in the psyches of most women that they can't even acknowledge their existence.

Trevor, however, didn't blame the women. In fact, he despised the men who preyed upon the irrationality of women. He hated men who fed upon a woman's inherent insecurities and manipulated them for their own personal gratification. To Trevor, women were a most precious treasure; to be honored, respected and treated like the queens. The smell of a woman's hair...the touch of her hand...the soft silky feel of her skin. For him women embodied all of the true beauty in the world. Trevor often quoted a line from a favorite movie where a man was asked how he knew that God existed. The man's reply was simple: "I'm sure there is a God because there are women." That pretty much summed it up for Trevor.

To Trevor's dismay, experience had taught him that most beautiful women were, at some point in their lives, tainted by the machinatons of nefarious men. This infestation ran deep and always seemed to manifest itself in some erratic behavior during his relationships with them. As he stroked her thigh softly in the palm of his hand, he wondered if this too would be the case with beautiful and tender Tori.

She applied the cream and then the bandage to Trevor's forehead, and pronounced, "There, good as new."

"Tori, you are one remarkable woman. I could rest here in your lap all night." He spoke in a soft and sincere tone.

She hesitated for a moment as if recalling some distant memory. "Everyone thought Sherry was the most beautiful girl in town. Everywhere we went guys would fall over each other to talk to her."

"I doubt she could hold a candle to you."

Tori leaned forward and kissed him on his forehead.

"What do you think happened to Sherry?" he asked.

"She was originally from Chicago and her parents still live there, so maybe she moved back home."

"When we first met you said you thought she disappeared... what made you say that?" Trevor was digging but tried not to sound like he was pressuring her.

"She and I were supposed to meet after her shift at the club one night, but she never showed up. I went by her apartment a few times, but she was never there, then about two days later I went by and found her door open and her apartment cleared out."

Trevor moved his fingers through her light sandy brown hair. "If we could only find her, I'm sure she could shed some light on things." He spoke out loud instinctively.

"Wait?" Tori lifted her head quickly. "She did say she had a sister living in Brookdale, but that they hadn't talked in years. They had some kind of disagreement that Sherry never wanted to talk about. She always said that her sister was very judgmental."

"Brookdale's only forty-five minutes away. Do you remember her sister's name?" Trevor asked, anticipating her answer.

"I do, but only because I thought it was kind of unique. Her name's Jade Simone, but by the way she acted whenever she spoke of her, I doubt that she would go live with her," Tori said with certainty. That name was vaguely familiar to Trevor but he just couldn't place it.

"When a person's in trouble and things get tight, you'd be surprised how quickly fences can be mended." Trevor thought of how he always somehow reconnected with Bruce during times of crisis, strengthening what was sometimes a tumultuous relationship between the two of them.

"You sound like you're speaking from experience," she hedged.

"I've known my share of hard times," Trevor said with sureness.

"Does that explain how you got that cut on your head and why there's a gun sitting on that box over there?"

Trevor sighed deeply and rubbed the palms of his hands over his face. "Okay, here it is: Earlier this evening I was paid a visit by who I'm assuming were the same two fools who told you to leave, except they were a bit less hospitable to me."

He grasped her hand and pulled her closer, gently resting his chin on her head. He told her everything that happened since he moved into the Hillcrest and, most importantly, of his suspicions. She listened intently, trying to grasp the magnitude of Trevor's words. It all seemed plausible to her, like a dream.

"I think we should try to find Sherry," Trevor said at the conclusion of his soliloquy.

"Why?" she asked inquisitively.

"I'm not sure, but something tells me that Sherry is the key to this whole thing."

HE AWOKE THE next morning, tired but with a renewed energy and focus. He had managed only a few hours of sleep. He and Tori had spent most of the night talking about his suspicions about the Hillcrest and trying to make sense of it all. Over the course of the night Trevor devised a plan. It was sketchy, light on detail, and required some extraneous variables to fall into place, but this was nothing new to him. He felt good to have some sense of direction; a roughed-out plan of action just like he had countless times before, but that didn't stop Trevor from feeling a copious amount of anxiety and stress.

Trevor was a schemer at heart; he had developed an ability to craft a plan of action despite having very little to go on. He relied on feel and instinct. He knew that he could craft an overarching and loosely defined plan then fill in the details as the variables started to come into play. A talent for doing this manifested itself at a very young age and over time he had honed this ability. By helping people in his neighborhood to resolve conflict, problems, and other issues. As word of his problem-solving capabilities started to grow, so did his reputation and street cred. His friends and complete strangers alike when facing dilemmas would often seek his counsel. He was Kid Fixit! He could assuage the fears, concerns, and apprehensions of those who sought him out. He would draw up a plan of action regardless of how little information or the number of roadblocks or obstacles to navigate.

They sat at the oval-shaped kitchen table and had breakfast: scrambled eggs, orange juice, and bagels. They agreed that the first step was to try and locate Tori's friend Sherry Simone. Tori pulled out a city directory from an open cardboard box on the floor in the kitchen and started thumbing through the pages. She stopped on a page and excitedly circled a Brookdale address with a red marker.

Jade Simone
157 Grove Avenue
Brookdale

Tori tore the page out and gave it to Trevor. Trevor's eyes focused on the name that she had circled in red.

"That's where I know that name from!" Trevor exclaimed. "She's an assistant DA. I read about her becoming the first black woman to reach that position in the DA's office."

"That makes sense because Sherry always said that her half-sister was very successful and had graduated from a prestigious law school," Tori replied.

After they finished eating Trevor decided to call Bruce and Rico. He asked Bruce to meet him in the front of the Hillcrest in an hour and hung up the phone. He knew that his conversation with Rico wouldn't be as succinct.

"Who is Tori and why do you want me to take her to Brookdale?" Rico questioned.

"Rico, I just need you to do me this favor and not ask a million questions like you always do," Trevor said, trying to move the conversation along.

"Is she fine?" Trevor could visualize Rico's broad smile on the other end of the phone.

"She's my girl, so you know that's the case, but that don't matter to you one way or the other right now."

"If you're saying that she's your girl Trev then she's gotta be super fine, fine as wine. Is she as fine as your old girl Monica?"

"Don't go there, Rico," Trevor said impatiently.

"Bet you hope she's not as crazy as that bitch either, huh? But boy was she fine. Fine as wine, that's what we 'usta say, right Trev?"

"Get serious Rico. I need your help. Can you do me this favor or not?" Trevor's tone tightened. A clear sign that his patience was running thin.

"Why didn't you call The Duke if you need help?"

"I did call Bruce and he's helping with something else, but I need your help on this Brookdale thing. Come on Rico, stop messing around. Are going to help me or what?"

"What's in it for me?"

"What do you need?"

"To start with, another job. Shit, I'm living on slave wages and I gotta get out of my mom's house soon. She's driving me crazy."

"So, what do you want? You want me to pay you for giving Tori a ride to Brookdale?" Trevor asked incredulously.

"No, man, but I do want you to help with my résumé like you promised a month ago."

"Rico, listen man, there's been some crazy shit going on. Tori will fill you in on the ride but I promise I'll help you with what you got to do as soon as things ease up for me. But straight up, I need you to help me with this right now!"

"Alright man, but remember everything's not just about you, Trev."

"I know Rico, I know."

"Okay, I'll be there in forty-five minutes."

Trevor hung up the phone and turned to Tori, who was still seated at the kitchen table. "Didn't sound like he was too anxious to take me to Brookdale," she said as she picked up her glass of orange juice.

"Rico's cool Tori, really! I've known him since grade school. He's just giving me a hard time because I haven't followed through on something I told him I would. But trust me; you're going to like him. Every girl I ever—"

Trevor stopped abruptly, knowing that he was about to put his foot in his mouth. But she showed no visible signs of picking up on his miscue, so he continued.

"...Plus it hasn't helped that he's been a little irritable because he's tired of living at his mom's house. You have to understand; I've always been there for him and lately with everything going on...well, I haven't really been there like I've been in the past."

"Sounds like you have a lot of people who are counting on you Mr. Stillwell."

Trevor sighed deeply. "Yeah, I guess so Tori. I just hope I don't let anyone down."

BRUCE MADE HIMSELF comfortable on the couch and grabbed the remote from the coffee table. The television noisily blared to life. "Yo, Trevor, the Bulls are playing tonight at 7:00. Jordan be ballin' his ass off."

"Man, how can you even think about watching a game with all this shit going on?"

"Welcome to my life," Bruce said in a hushed tone.

Trevor didn't respond verbally, but looked inquisitively at Bruce.

Bruce was using the remote to channel surf. "So, what our next move...damn I thought the Bulls were coming on, Trev?"

"Bruce do you want to hear about the plan I devised to try and pull our asses out of the fire or watch Jordan light up the Knicks?"

"Don't be a smart-ass Trevor and as your college educated ass would say the two are mutually exclusive," barked Bruce.

Trevor decided to leave well enough alone and not to respond to his comment. He grabbed a white wife-beater, a lavender short-sleeve polo shirt, a pair of boxer briefs, and a pair of beige khaki shorts out of the green plastic laundry bin on his kitchen table. "Let me jump in the shower then we'll talk. Besides, I am waiting for Tori and Rico to call from Brookdale. Whether my plan has any chance of success depends entirely on what they find in there."

"Rico, so what is Big Boy doing for you, and how's your little chippy fit into all of this?" Bruce asked, but again Trevor said nothing. He was lost in his own thoughts as he headed to the bathroom to shower.

Bruce noticed the package containing the unopened lock Trevor bought the other night. "I knew you was thinkin' more 'bout that ass last night more then you let on," Bruce mumbled out loud as he reclined on the couch. Stretching out his body he gave a big yawn. "I knew that girl's pussy had you open." Bruce heard the shower being turned on and realized that he was talking to himself and that Trevor hadn't heard a word.

The water from the shower climbed from warm to hot, and the steam ensconced the bathroom in a heavy white mist. Trevor leaned heavily against the wall of the shower directly below the showerhead. The water pelted off his head and cascaded down his face like rain down a windowpane. He felt the angst and anxiety which had been his closest companions the past forty-eight hours slowly subside down the drain along with the excess water. As he relaxed, his thoughts drifted to Tori and how her body seemed to fit so comfortably within his arms like interconnecting pieces of a puzzle. He knew that if he had her with him in that shower, he would surely wish the rest of the world away.

Bruce was fast asleep; his body was sprawled out on the couch. Trevor wondered how Bruce could sleep comfortably with his body contorted in such a manner.

"Oh well, to each his own, I guess," Trevor said to himself. He dressed, placed the gun on the coffee table beside the remote control then made himself comfortable on the burgundy recliner next to the couch.

He looked at the lock and thought about doing what he had intended to do the other night when he bought it, but sleep came calling.

THE HILLCREST DAMSELS

BROOKDALE WAS A picturesque landscape of tree-lined streets and colorful gardens. A community of quiet winding streets, well-manicured lawns and flowering red calla lily gardens. Rico turned his jeep onto Grover Avenue where large willowy trees lined the sidewalks, allowing only a hint of the soft shadowy sunlight to trickle into view. They pulled up to a gray cottage with a dark purple front door.

"Well, I guess we're here, Rico," Tori said after verifying the address that she had written on a piece of paper.

"You're right Tori." Rico pulled the jeep over.

She took a deep breath and opened the car door. "Wait, I'm coming with you," Rico demanded.

"No Rico. You should probably stay here. You can watch me from the car. I'll be fine. If she is here, I don't want to overwhelm her."

Rico was about to try to refute that point but she quickly exited the jeep before he could say another word. She opened the gate in the picket fence, traveled along a cobblestone path to the stairs and rang the bell, which she noticed was encased in an intricately crafted metal faceplate with the initials J.S.

As Rico looked at Tori standing on the porch, he thought about the conversation they had along the way. He wasn't sure he believed Trevor's suspicions about the Hillcrest, but he also knew from experience that Trevor was a very astute, intuitive, and rational brother. He was as grounded a brother as Rico had ever known. But Trevor's suspicions seemed to him like something straight out of a movie script. As Tori waited patiently at the door, she glanced back at him and bravely smiled.

The door opened slowly. No words were exchanged as they just stood and stared at one another. A tear welled in the corner of the eye of the richly colored, brown skinned woman standing at the doorway. "Oh Tori, I've missed you so much." Tori didn't respond verbally but her shoulders relaxed slightly. "I'm sorry that I had to leave you like that, but I was so scared." The woman completely broke down and reached out to embrace her. They hugged as Sherry cried uncontrollably.

"It's okay Sherry." She spotted a bench with two large sunflower pots at the opposite end of the porch. "Come on and sit over here and talk." It took Sherry five minutes to regain her composure.

"I was really worried about you." Tori's tone was comforting. Sherry could sense her genuine concern.

"I know Tori and I'm sorry. I just couldn't deal with it anymore. I had to leave. I'm sorry for not telling you what was really going on but I had no choice."

"Sherry, it's okay. I'm here for you but you have to tell me everything you know and I mean everything. It's very important."

"Why?"

"Well, I met this guy. His name is Trevor Stillwell and I think he can help us."

THE PHONE RANG and a startled Trevor practically jumped up off the recliner on the first ring. He looked over at Bruce who was sound asleep. "Hello?" His voice was raspy.

"Trevor it's me. What's wrong with your voice? Were you sleeping?"

"Yeah, I fell asleep after taking a shower. How did you make out?" Despite being a little groggy there was still excitement in his voice.

"That depends on how you look at it. I found Sherry, in fact, she's sitting right here with me. You were right, she was at her sister's."

"Really?"

"Really, and that's not all. She had plenty to tell me about the Hillcrest, Arthur Baxter, Mateo and the club…" She hesitated.

"And?"

"And you were right, she ran to her sister's because she was scared of Mateo. And she knew her sister as an assistant DA could offer her protection."

"How much does Sherry's sister know?"

"Sherry has not told her sister what happened but she was going to as soon as she got her bearings. All that she told her was that she ran into some financial problems and needed somewhere to stay."

"So, her sister doesn't know what's happening at the Hillcrest."

"Sherry said that she didn't tell her anything about that yet."

"Why?"

"Trevor, she's been through a lot and she's scared."

"I understand, I guess. Where's her sister at now?"

"Work of course. According to Sherry that's all her sister does with her life. All work and no play."

"Ask Sherry if her sister ever brings work home or ever works from home or has a home office."

Tori put the phone down and walked over to Sherry, who was curled up on the living room sofa. A minute later she returned to the phone. "She said yes, in fact her sister has an office set up in the basement."

"Okay, where is Rico?"

"He is in the kitchen. Sherry made him a sandwich."

"Figures. Put him on the phone."

A few seconds passed. "Yo, what's up Trevor?"

"Rico, put the food down. And let's get back to business," Trevor barked from the other end of the line.

"It's not like that Trevor. Besides, all I've been doing is sitting around with nothing to do waiting on you," pleaded Rico.

"Whatever Rico. Maybe it's me; I know that I am under a lot of stress."

"I guess that could be interpreted as an apology. You asked me to drive Tori here and watch her back. Well, mission accomplished. So, instead of you getting mad because I was raiding Sherry's sister's refrigerator you should be saying 'Thank you Rico.'"

"You got a point Rico. Goods job...so far. Now here is what I need you to do next and pay careful attention because whether or not I get out of this mess unscathed depends on how well you execute this part of the plan."

Trevor spent the next ten minutes explaining the plan and what he needed Rico to do.

"Can you do it Rico?" Trevor asked.

"Not a problem."

"Okay, call me as soon as you find it."

"Are you sure it will be there?"

"If she has a legit extension of her work office in the basement then she's got to have it there."

"Okay Trev, if you say so."

"Get to work man, and put Tori back on the phone."

"Hello Trevor. I miss you." She expected him to say the same but the line was silent. "Trevor, did you hear me? Trevor are you there? Trevor!"

Dial tone.

THE PISTOL WAS positioned firmly under Trevor's right armpit, pushing against his ribcage. He instinctively recoiled, moving slightly in the opposite direction of the cold steel pressed against his side.

"Put the phone down punk ass nigga and move over to the couch. Wake up your boy over there too." He didn't have to see who was holding the pistol, the voice was unmistakable. "Go on! Wake him up!"

Trevor placed the phone down on its base and slowly walked toward the couch. Glancing down at the table, he noticed that the gun he had placed there was missing. *What the fuck! Where did it go?* he thought to himself.

Trevor reached down and slowly nudged Bruce awake. "Yo man...yo, man," Trevor was careful not to use Bruce's name. "Wake up, we got problems man."

Bruce opened his eyes and looked around the room and saw the man he pummeled yesterday standing there holding a pistol on him and Trevor. "Damn it, I knew I shouldn't have fell asleep man," he said in a voice slightly above a whisper as he shifted into a seated position on the couch. He slowly raised his eye level until he was looking eye to eye with his adversary.

"Go on, take a seat." The man gestured for Trevor to move by waving the barrel of his pistol in a sharp, deliberate motion.

Trevor sat next to Bruce on the couch. Bruce rubbed his eyes and for the first time since encountering the man in the red Nike sweat suit the day before, he had a good look at his adversary. The man was clean-shaven, including his head, and had wiry sharp eyebrows that connected over the bridge of his nose. The skin around his eyes and cheeks were puffy and irritated, no doubt the result of the pummeling Bruce inflicted on him in the hallway of Trevor's apartment, but he somehow seemed none the worse for wear. He appeared almost comfortable wearing a battered face. Although he had a much smaller frame than his simian-like partner from the day before, he was by no means a frail man. He stood roughly six feet tall, and even dressed in a baggy sweat suit, appeared well built and sturdy. Bruce estimated him to be a solid 160 pounds.

A scowl stained his face as he spoke. "Listen up you two punk ass niggas! This is what we're gonna do. You gonna get up…very fuckin' slowly…and I mean very fuckin' slowly, and walk down to the super's office in the basement. I'll be right behind you and if either of you tries sumthin' stupid, I won't hesitate to put a cap in your ass. You best believe dat. Especially you!" His eyes narrowed into a stern gaze directed at Bruce. "There will be a round two for you and me, you can bet the house and kids on that."

Bruce responded with an evil smile that displayed the fury in his soul.

Again, the man motioned with the barrel of the gun for them to get up and start walking toward the door.

As they walked down the stairs Bruce spoke to Trevor in a voice barely audible, rising slightly above a whisper. "How did he get the drop on us? Did you answer the door?"

Trevor looked questioningly at Bruce. "Of course not! He had a key."

"So you were right about someone having a key to your apartment, but you know he wouldn't have gotten the drop on us if you changed the lock stead of tappin' that ass last night."

Trevor didn't respond; he just cut his eyes disapprovingly in Bruce's direction.

"I'll tell you what, why don't both of you shut the fuck up and just keep hands behind your back and walk!"

The nameplate was black with engraved silver lettering: Arthur Baxter – Property Manager. "Go head, knock on the door," the man said in a menacing voice. The voice emanated from several feet behind them, Trevor could tell that he was keeping a safe distance as they stood by the door. If they tried anything, he would have ample time to aim and shoot.

Bruce knocked firmly. "Who is it?" The voice behind the door sounded strained and annoyed.

"It's me Arty! Open the fuckin' door!" the man with the gun shouted in a bellicose and annoyed voice.

"It's unlocked!"

"You heard the man, open the door and go in." Trevor could see that Bruce was growing tired of taking commands from this man. He also knew that Bruce sometimes got reckless when he was annoyed so Trevor had to stay on top of this situation to keep his friend from doing something reckless.

The room was dimly lit. The only light emanated from a small lamp stationed on a wooden office desk, crowded with papers and located in the center of the room. Seated behind the desk was a weary looking black man with black wire-rimmed glasses and jean overalls. The man leaped from his seat as Bruce and Trevor entered the room. "Why'd you bring them here Moe? I thought you and Roscoe were handling this thing!"

"Sit down and be cool Arty, Roscoe didn't show so I had to bring 'em down here. I need your help tying them up and getting them to the car." Moe closed the door after he entered with a backwards thrust of his foot. Bruce and Trevor stopped and stood near the corner of the desk.

"I'm not getting involved in this Moe." Arty shook his head violently and pointed at them as he spoke.

"You already involved Arty my boy. When you in bizness with Mateo you don't decide what you gonna do and what you not gonna—" Moe was interrupted by a loud knock on the door that startled both he and Arty. Trevor recognized that knock; he'd heard that same knock only a day earlier.

Moe instinctively turned the pistol toward the door. Trevor immediately looked at Bruce, whom he knew would seize any opportunity to attack. Recognizing his mistake, Moe quickly refocused the pistol and his attention on Bruce and Trevor. "Don't even think about it. Move over by the window." They both took a few steps backward and rested against the wall under a small rectangular basement window.

"Who is it?" Moe barked a loud voice.

"It's me Moe."

He opened the door with his free hand. A look of recognition engulfed Moe's face. "Where the fuck have you been Roscoe?"

Roscoe entered the room. He was a mountain of a man. Trevor estimated Roscoe to be at least six feet six and weighing in excess of two hundred and seventy pounds. He had broad shoulders and a square face. A large circular bandage was displayed prominently on his forehead and his right eye and lips were bruised and noticeably swollen. "I was waiting in the parking lot—"

Roscoe stop abruptly as his attention was drawn to Bruce and Trevor. Instantly his face tensed and contorted with rage. "Dattttt'sssss the mutherfucker who sssnuck me!" he hissed. Without another word, he charged toward Bruce with the force of an enraged bull. Fueled by an uncontrollable rage that was solidly etched on his face.

"Roscoe, wait, no!" Moe's plea fell on deaf ears.

Bruce only had a spilt second to act before Roscoe would be on him. Instead of retreating or taking a defensive stance, Bruce took a step toward the hard charging giant. Bruce lowered his body and executed a perfect side kick. The ball of his foot impacted solidly with the soft cartilage of Roscoe's knee. A sickening *POP!*

was heard followed by a loud scream. The first was the sound of Roscoe's kneecap disengaging from his patellar tendon; the second was Roscoe's response to the rush of pain he felt. Roscoe was stopped in his tracks and slowly tumbled forward.

Moe was aiming his pistol at Bruce but Roscoe's lumbering body obscured his view. Bruce stayed low and kept Roscoe's body between him and Moe. Bruce quickly rose up, and hit Roscoe with his shoulder like tackling a dummy during a football blocking drill. Bruce completely reversed Roscoe's momentum and propelled Roscoe backwards. Roscoe fell backwards and slammed into Moe, who didn't have time to react. The force of their impact sent both men careening into a large wooden table which shattered upon their impact. As they both lay prostrate on the floor, Trevor found a light switch on the wall and quickly illuminated the darkened room.

Slightly dazed, Moe slowly stood and regained his footing only to find Bruce standing a few feet away, pointing a gun squarely at him. Trevor slowly shook head in amazement. *Bruce must have taken the gun off the coffee table while I slept and before Moe entered the apartment.*

"Yo, I am not messin' around, you should drop your piece now! Or I'll end it for you, with the quickness!" Bruce demanded. The fall had not dislodged the gun from Moe's hand; it rested loosely there. While Bruce had his gun trained on Moe's chest. Moe knew that by the time he tightened his grip and raised his hand to take aim, Bruce would have gotten off two rounds. He wisely decided to drop the gun on the floor.

"Good decision, Moe. That is your name, isn't it, Moe? I didn't want to hafta put ya down but I'm glad you know I would've. Now slide that piece over here." Moe started to bend down to reach for the gun.

"Don't even think about it. Kick it over to me." The gun slid on the smooth surface of the floor and stopped a few inches in front of Trevor.

Bruce handed Trevor the gun that he was holding. Trevor grabbed it and held it securely with both hands, putting Moe directly within its crosshairs. Bruce removed a handkerchief from his back pocket. He used it to retrieve Moe's gun from the floor. After carefully wiping down the gun in a meticulous fashion, he examined it closely. "Yo, Moe this is a nice piece, do you mind if I keep it," he said in a snide tone. The message was clear he was keeping the gun and there wasn't a damn thing Moe, Roscoe, or anyone else could do about it.

Arty who hadn't said a word or moved a muscle since Roscoe entered the room, sat silently, sweating profusely. It looked as though he had taken a shower fully dressed. Sweat glistened on his dark skin and pooled on his forehead like raindrops on a freshly paved road. His nappy unkempt hair absorbed whatever sweat didn't make it to his forehead. He was transfixed by the events of the last few minutes, seemingly unable to wipe the sweat from his own face. Roscoe was crouched in the corner of the room holding his disfigured leg and moaning quietly. Moe stood next to him, not seeming to know what to do next.

"What's our next move Trevor? It's on you man." Bruce spoke calmly and confidently.

Trevor, on the other hand, knew that if he tried to speak his voice would tremble—laced with the nervous tension that was running rampant throughout his body. So, he decided to wait until his heart, which had been racing furiously and now was firmly lodged in his throat, slowed its pace. He tried to focus his thoughts and concentrate on the situation at hand. He felt like he was trying to wake from a bad dream. He was fatigued and lightheaded but knew he would have to get it together and get it together fast. There was much at stake.

"Trev, you can put the gun down." Bruce reached out and touched Trevor's arm to gently push it down.

"I got them covered." Bruce pointed Moe's gun squarely at his adversary's chest.

Bruce continued. "Put it away. We don't want any accidents to happen. So, what's next Trev?"

Trevor started to get his composure back. As the pounding in his head subsided he could feel things slowing down to a normal speed. With his head clear he began to refocus on the situation at hand. He swallowed hard to clear his throat before speaking. "Do you have keys to that utility closet down in the basement?" Trevor directed his words and stare at the man seated behind the desk.

Arty nodded robotically, removed a set of keys from the desk door, took off a large silver key and threw it to Trevor.

He caught the key and handed it to Bruce. "There is a storage room in the basement right next to the boiler room. Lock them up in there. It's not that big but it's secure and should hold them for a while anyway. And Bruce, please try not to shoot either of them."

"I ain't making any promises on that one Trev," Bruce said with a wry smile etched on a stone face.

Bruce motioned to Moe to get up.

Moe helped Roscoe to his feet. Roscoe cried out in pain a few times on his way out of the room. Each time Bruce told him to suck it up and keep moving. The door closed and Trevor approached Arty. He pulled up a chair and sat at the opposite end of the desk. Making sure to display the gun as a show of his authority over the situation.

"So where do we go from here?" Trevor asked after exhaling for what felt like the first time all day.

"Listen, I don't want any trouble," Arty said nervously.

"That's good because neither do I, although it seems that we both have some anyway. It's really up to you and me how far this thing goes," Trevor said confidently.

Arty tried to lean back in his chair. "Keep your hands on the desk where I can see them, Mr. Baxter."

He straightened up and placed his hands in view for Trevor.

"You have me at a disadvantage, you know my name but I don't know yours."

"Sure you do Mr. Baxter." Arty looked perplexedly at Trevor.

"My name is Kim Stillwell, but I normally go by my middle name, Trevor. Kim stands for Kimbro. I was named after my granddaddy who was a Tuskegee Airman. Kim can also be short for Kimberly, but I'm definitely not a woman."

"I'll be damned." Arty shook his head in disbelief.

"You see Mr. Baxter; a few months ago I was offered a job with a company here in town. They helped me transition from college to the world of working folks and that included helping me find an apartment. A woman from their office was assigned to help me with all the logistics stuff. Her name is Karen Stillson. She did all the groundwork for me while I finished tying up some personal loose ends on campus, so I'm assuming you somehow confused her with the name on the application; after all K. Stillson is very similar to K. Stillwell. And Karen was an attractive, unmarried woman, just perfect for the little hustle Mateo's got going here at the Hillcrest.

"So Arty why don't you just tell me what this whole thing at the Hillcrest is all about?"

There was a long silence. "I'm waiting." Another few seconds passed. "I think it would be easier for you to talk to me rather than my friend, who you just saw wreck that Roscoe fella, don't you?"

Arty clearly understood the intent of Trevor's warning, and figured at this point he had nothing to lose. He started to spill his guts. "I wasn't there when the apartment was leased to you. I was out of town the day it was shown to you, or I guess it was Miss Stillson, or whomever. I had my nephew Stephen show her the apartment."

Trevor jumped in. "And he reported back to you that the woman he showed the apartment to was attractive, single, and moving in alone. She seemed to match the profile, so you leased the apartment to Kim Stillwell thinking that Karen's name was Kim. Or something like that, right?"

"That's it pretty much. My stupid nephew screwed this whole thing up. So that's how you ended up living at the Hillcrest. Can I go now?" Arty replied.

"What? C'mon Arty. We're just getting started." Trevor's head was completely clear now.

"Do you own the Hillcrest?" Arty nodded affirmatively.

"Okay, here's what I don't understand. Why are you allowing Mateo to use the Hillcrest as his own private farm club to recruit women for his high-class prostitution ring? Honestly, you seem like a decent guy."

After a short silence Trevor continued, "Are you two partners or something?"

"HELL NO!" Arty almost jumped out of his seat as he responded. Trevor realized he had hit a nerve and decided to press a little harder.

"It sure looks like you two are partners."

"I don't care what it looks or sounds like, we're not. Never have been, never will be!"

"I know you got more to say about that, right?" Trevor nonchalantly nudged at the gun again for him to see. The nonverbal message was clear to Arty.

He sighed deeply and looked down at the desk before speaking. "I know Mateo from Edgewood. I usta place bets with him, and over time got a little in the hole with him. A few years ago my mother died and left me the Hillcrest. I came here with the intent of selling it, paying off my debt to Mateo and moving to Florida with the rest of the money. I had a buyer all lined up and everything when Mateo showed up and completely changed my plans." Trevor knew exactly who that would-be buyer was but said nothing.

Arty became more emotional as his story unfolded. "My mother was a saint; God rest her soul. She didn't care about making a lot of money. She could've made a mint renting these apartments for top dollar, but instead she rented them at fair market price and most below market prices, just enough of them to make ends meet. A handful of the units she would dedicate as temporary housing for wayward women—you know, teenage runaways, battered and abused women, and women ex-cons trying to get back on the straight and narrow.

"Shit, when Mateo found this out it was like leading a fox to the hen house. In a month's time he had manipulated most of those poor vulnerable women into traveling back and forth to Edgewood to work the streets for him."

"Why did he have them running to all the way to Edgewood, why not put them on the streets here?" Trevor asked inquisitively.

"Law enforcement around here was too heavy. The DA is tough here. Mateo's as bold and as mean as they get but he's terrified of the DA. Turns out that some DA in some backwater town in Louisiana put Mateo's daddy away for life when he was a teenager. And as much as he hates the law enforcement, he's terrified of facing the same fate as his daddy. Shit, the DA runs such a tight ship 'round here that Mateo couldn't even pay off the street vice cops. So that's when he got the idea about the club." Did *Sherry know of Mateo's fear of the DA? Is that's why she fled to her sister's?* Trevor thought. Whatever the case this information was exactly what he needed to confirm that his plan was on point.

"Now we're getting somewhere Arty. Tell me about the Fox Trot," Trevor said in eager anticipation.

Arty's initial reluctance to talk was melting away. This was his chance to lessen the burden he had been carrying for so long. "Mateo thought opening a gentlemen's club to prostitute women was less risky than parading them on the street and having to deal with the cops. He could also stay off the DA's radar. Mateo found that there is a huge demand for discreet high-end prostitution in this town among married doctors, lawyers, businessmen and other professionals. This was his chance to move from an average street hustler to a big-time player. He wanted the club to be an elegant joint, for it to look like some kind of Arabian place, but he's got no class and absolutely no business sense. He spent all the money on cars, his wardrobe, and whatever before the renovations were completed. Shit, the club is only half finished."

"So, you fronted the club for him?"

"I took a second mortgage on the Hillcrest to buy the club. He said that once the club started making some money, he would let me out free and clear. Then I'd sell the Hillcrest and move on like I wanted to do from jump. So, you see, we're not partners in the illegal stuff, just the property."

"Is that what you tell yourself to sleep at night? And do you really think that he would let you out of this thing just like that?"

Trevor let his words hang in the air for a minute before speaking again. "What are you into Mateo for?"

Arty hesitated for a moment. "Twenty large more or less."

"And how much did you pay for the building where the Fox Trot is located?"

"What are you going to do—prepare my balance sheet?" Arty asked sarcastically.

Trevor could tell that Arty was becoming emotionally drained. Their conversation was taking a toll on him. Trevor decided to take a more compassionate approach now that he had broken him down.

"Arty, I need to know because believe it or not I may be able to help you."

Arty's expression changed from exhaustion to surprise. "How you gonna to do that?"

"Leave that up to me, but I do need to know more," Trevor pleaded.

Trevor's body language and speech were disarming and relaxed. He wanted more information and knew that he would have to be more cajoling than threatening.

"I paid twenty thousand for all three buildings. I bought them cheap at a city tax sale. Another twenty thousand was s'pose to be spent for the build-out for the club, which still ain't complete because like I said he spent most of it on other things. He doesn't know how to run no club! Just because he makes some money pimping and runs a profitable book in Edgewood, he thinks he's fuckin' head of Time Warner or somthin."

It was obvious to Trevor that Arty was not a fan of Mateo, more than likely even a reluctant participant. Trevor was starting to feel sympathetic toward the bespectacled black man seated across from him. He had been carrying a heavy burden.

"So, when a woman who was carefully screened to live at the Hillcrest decided she didn't want to work at the club, what happened?" Trevor was anxious for confirmation of all his suspicions.

"Mateo would start pressuring her. First he'd try to cut off her source of primary income," Arty replied.

"Like getting her fired from her job?" Trevor said in an agitated tone.

"Yeah that's right but how did you know that?"

"A little birdy told me." *A birdy named Tori,* Trevor thought to himself.

"Tell me how the whole thing worked," Trevor asked in a very non-threatening tone.

"You obviously know that Sassafras is a hot area. Everyone wants to live here, and the Hillcrest is a beautiful building with its ornate architecture, high ceilings, large windows and historic appeal, so when we started advertising the space we got inundated with applications."

Trevor could tell by the timbre of his voice that Arty was proud of the Hillcrest, its aesthetic and the neighborhood.

"Of course, Mateo tossed out all the male or couple applications from the start then he looked at the remaining women and scored them on a scale of 1 to 10 based on appearance and vulnerability. We got photos of all the female applicants to judge their attractiveness.

"Those with the highest score were the ones he had me offer apartments to. They were attractive but most of all vulnerable. Some didn't have steady work or didn't have a support mechanism like family or close friends living in the state, whatever Mateo thought he could capitalize on."

"But I never sent a picture in with my application...oh wait, I do remember now. Karen wanted to get me to take a picture for the application which I though was illegal and stupid, so I jokingly told Karen to send in a picture of herself. Guess she really did. And I guess that only helped to solidify that she was the person who would be renting Apartment 3A. That she was Kim Stillwell." The series of events that lead to Trevor being at the Hillcrest and the events of the past few days all seemed surreal to Trevor.

"What also helped was a girl had just hastily moved out and Mateo was very upset about that. I don't know why but he wanted that apartment rented to another fish as soon as possible." Arty stopped abruptly.

Sherry, Trevor thought to himself.

"Fish?" asked Trevor.

"Yeah, that's what Mateo called women in the Hillcrest. Fish. Fish in a fishbowl just waiting for him to come scoop them up."

"Damn that's fucked up. And you just sat back and let this whole thing happen on your watch in your building." Trevor shook his head in disgust.

"You'd be surprised how much control you can get over a person just from the information they willingly give you in a tenant application," Arty said.

Arty continued, "Mateo is a pimp, a hustler and hard as

nails. I can't fuck with him, plus I have a heart condition and he knows that. Look, we are still getting applications even though we don't have any apartments available." Arty picked up a bunch of applications piled on his desk.

"If the girl had a job then Mateo would call their bosses or send a letter with suggestive pictures of them working at the club. Once they were without a job and low on cash, they became more receptive to working the club. He would let them live rent-free at the Hillcrest if they worked the club. After a while he would manipulate them into pulling a trick or two on the side and before long, they were full-fledged prostitutes, making money hand-over-fist for him.

"If a woman refused his offer, he would just send Moe and Roscoe by to get them to move out quickly so that he could get another fish in and start the process all over again. See, Mateo's philosophy is that every woman has a little 'ho' in her and that under the right circumstances he could bring it out of them. He turned my mother's Hillcrest into some kind of prostitution laboratory. Can you believe that? He's a really sick fucker." Arty breathed deeply and leaned hard against the back of his chair, causing it to creak loudly. Soon the tears flowed steadily down the cheeks of his furrowed face.

They sat in silence for more than a few minutes. Although Trevor felt somewhat vindicated, he still couldn't believe all this had been going on at the Hillcrest. "You're part of this too Arty," Trevor said with a disgusted looked.

"It may look that way, but I'm not. I've helped many women get away from him at my own risk. He just has me over a barrel here, there's not much I can do," Arty said as he wiped his face dry.

"Well, here's what you can do. You can set up a meeting with Mateo."

"For the three of us?" Arty said with more than a slight sense of concern.

"No, just him and me."

"What do I tell him it's about?"

"Tell him it's about a business proposition."

"Are you sure you know what you're getting into?"

"Don't worry about that Arty, that's my problem now."

"Don't forget I still own the property...at least on paper..." Arty's words trailed off as he realized what little difference his ownership made in light of Mateo's corrupting influence and his head sagged into his shoulders.

"Arty, do you still want to go to Florida?"

"What?"

"You said that your original plan was to sell the Hillcrest and move to Florida, do you still want to do that?" Trevor asked confidently.

Arty looked confusedly at him and stammered out a response. "I-I-I guess so, I just haven't thought about it in a while...but how the hell's that gonna happen now?"

"You let me worry about that. Here's what I need you to do." Trevor leaned forward in his chair, closing the distance between the two. He spoke slowly and deliberately as the shadows of the fading sun enveloped the room. Arty listened intently, occasionally nodding in agreement.

Bruce entered the room. Both Trevor and Arty jumped slightly. "Calm down, it's just me."

Bruce sat in a chair near the shattered table's remains while Arty and Trevor huddled over the desk. Whatever Trevor was saying caused Arty to grin and nod in agreement.

RRIIINNNGG! **TREVOR ENTERED** his apartment to the sound of the telephone. "Hello...Hello?" He answered the phone hoping that it was Tori on the other end. Trevor's mind was racing, still mulling over the conversation with Arty.

"Trevor! ...Oh...thank God it's you! Are you alright? I've been calling you for the last three hours! What happened? Where were you? You hung up so abruptly I thought something happened to you." Tori spoke hysterically in one long rambling sentence.

"Calm down Tori, I'm okay and I'll explain what happened later but for now I want you to stay there with Sherry for a while. I don't want you coming back here," Trevor said in a stern tone.

"What? What do you mean?" she confusedly replied. "Are you in danger?"

"I'm serious! I want you to ask Sherry if you can stay there for a few days, until I go to get you."

"Why? What's wrong? What happened? Are you okay?" Tori's questions came in rapid succession.

Trevor sensed that she was becoming more frantic and tried his best to assuage her. "Tori relax, I'm cool. Really. It's just that things are happening more quickly than I expected and I don't want you around here until things settle down."

There was a brief silence but when she next spoke, she was

slightly calmer. Her discontent with his responses was palpable. "When will I see you?"

"In a day or so, I'll go and pick you up on Sunday," Trevor replied.

"On Sunday?" she asked disappointedly. "Trevor I haven't met Sherry's sister and you want me to ask her to let me stay here until Sunday."

"If you can't then tell Rico I said to take you to a hotel. Tell him I said to use the credit card I gave him for emergencies."

"You gave him a credit card? For what kind of emergencies? Did you know this was going to happen? Are you in some kind of trouble?"

"Tori...please...calm down! I have a lot to tell you but the main point is I don't want you coming back here until I go get you." Trevor could hear her struggling to hold back the tears.

"Regardless of what happens Tori, I'll be there on Sunday. I promise." Trevor tried his best to sound firm and convincing, but the shakiness of his voice betrayed him. He could feel her anxiety; it reminded him of the first time they met at Sal's. He couldn't believe that was only a few days ago. After everything that happened it felt like a lifetime ago.

"Listen Tori, everything's going to be okay, baby girl. Trust me. God willing this whole thing will be over soon and I'll come pick you up on Sunday. I need you to listen to me and be strong, okay?"

Bruce walked into the apartment and coughed in order to get Trevor's attention. Slightly startled, Trevor turned quickly and reached for the gun he had placed at the small of his back. Bruce raised his hands in mock surrender. Bruce smiled and pointed to the bathroom. Trevor frowned and nodded his head.

"Tori, I know that you're worried, but things are coming together, it's going to be okay. I promise!" Trevor knew that he was as uncertain about the future as ever but tried his best to mask his concern.

"Alright," she said disappointedly.

"That's my baby girl, now how did you make out?" Trevor said calmly.

"Rico did find some office letterhead in her desk in the office but he made such a mess I had to go down and straight up after him. I thought you said he had done this kind of thing—"

Trevor interrupted her and spoke excitedly. "You found blank letterhead. Official letterhead from the DA's office. Does it have an official imprimatur of the attorney general's office?"

"Yes, I think so."

"Is it a seal that is imprinted on the letterhead like when you have something notarized?"

"YES!!! It has the DA's name, logo, stamp and address. But I still don't understand why a blank page piece of letterhead is going to help us."

"Tori, it is more than important, it's the coup de grâce, baby girl," Trevor excitedly said.

"I just don't understand."

"Don't worry Tori. I promise to explain everything very soon, okay?"

She reluctantly agreed. "Okay, Trevor."

"I'll tell Rico to take you a nice hotel."

"You don't want me to see if I can stay here?"

"No, never mind. I'll have Rico take you to the Radisson on Burke."

"But I don't have a change of clothes or even a toothbrush."

"Tori, use the credit card to buy whatever you need. It's only till Sunday. Please baby, work with me on this."

"Okay Trevor."

"I promise that everything's going to be okay." That was the second time he made that promise. He was trying to convince himself as much as comfort her.

"Alright Trevor," she said bravely as her lips curled into a halfhearted smile on the other end of the phone.

"I'll call you at the hotel as soon as I can."

"Bye Trevor and please be careful." She handed the phone to Rico and turned away and took a deep breath.

Trevor filled Rico in on what had transpired and asked him to get back to pick him up at the Hillcrest after taking Tori to the Radisson and setting her up there.

"I got you Trevor. I'll be there right after I make sure Tori has everything she needs." Rico spoke like a man who was taking charge of the situation.

Trevor hung up the phone then quickly dialed a number he had committed to memory many weeks earlier. Bruce came out of the bathroom and rested on the couch. "Mont Marketing, where can I direct your call?" the woman on the other end said dryly.

"Mr. Marvin Moncrieff, special extension 55 please."

"One moment please."

Trevor walked to the window and looked down upon the street. He watched Arty and Moe helping Roscoe into a cab. They exchanged a few heated words before Moe disappeared into the cab. Arty stood motionless for a moment then, as if sensing Trevor's glare, he looked up at the window of Trevor's apartment. Their eyes met, and Trevor slowly nodded.

"Hello Marvin Montcreif, here."

"Hello Mr. Moncrieff, it's Trevor Stillwell."

"Trevor, I'm getting ready for an important client meeting, can we talk later?"

"This will only take a minute and it's very time sensitive."

"Fair enough, what's going on?"

"Are you still interested in acquiring the Hillcrest?"

"THIS OFFICE IS off-da-hook, Trevor!" Rico stood in the center of the room looking around in amazement. He walked over and ran his hand along the surface of the dark mahogany desk where Trevor was seated.

"You know Sherry almost caught me nosing around her sister's stuff!" Rico exclaimed.

"Really. You weren't exactly stealthy now were you?"

"What you are talking about Trev?" Rico gave him a perplexed glare.

"I heard you made a mess of her office looking for the letterhead and that Tori had to go put everything back together and clean up the disaster you left behind you."

"It was tough, man. I was trying to be stealthy, so I didn't turn on any lights; all I had was the light that came through those small ass basement windows. And I was under the gun because I knew that Tori could only distract Sherry for a short time. And to make things worse, she had tons of files, papers and shit down there. She must work her ass off if she has to bring that much work home."

"She's an assistant DA for the entire state, not just a city or town or region. That's no joke. She must put in twelve-hour days and weekends on the regular," Trevor replied.

Rico moved from the desk to the window and felt the fabric

of the rich rust colored drapes between his fingers. "I wish my sheets were made out of this stuff, it's so soft and velvety."

Trevor twisted his expression and looked up from behind the computer screen. "What the hell are you talking about man?"

"I don't know man; I guess I'm just a little nervous. I tend to ramble a little when I'm nervous," Rico said as he turned and walked to the far end of the room.

"You're telling me like I don't already know that. Rico, we've been friends since grade school. Shoot, I know all your idiosyncrasies and peccadillos."

"All my what? Trev, fuck, dumb that shit down a little. You must be pretty nervous too because you always start using your big college vocabulary when you're nervous!"

Rico was right; despite his cool outward demeanor inside he was a mess, full of self-doubt and anxiety. *Who do I think I am? I got my ass kicked, a gun stuck in my side and now I got to run a con on this pimp who thinks he is Kingpin of Crime. I'll be supremely lucky to get out of this thing unscathed.* Trevor's mind was racing out of control.

"Trev, whatcha doing with that letterhead anyway?"

"Working on the master plan, my rotund friend." Trevor smiled from behind the computer screen.

"I see, the master plan, huh? Well how 'bout shining some light on it for me. After all I only took your girl to Brookdale, stole letterhead from Sherry's sister for you, and deposited your girl safely at the Radisson. I think I deserve to know what you've got planned."

Trevor stopped typing and gave Slop his full attention for the first time since entering the office. "Okay Rico Albert Cubberson, what do you want to know?"

"For starters, how did you know that Sherry's sister worked for the DA?"

"Tori mentioned that Sherry had a sister and I remembered her name from a newspaper article on her appointment as the first black woman assistant DA ever in the state," Trevor replied.

"And?" Rico wanted to know everything.

"Tori and I figured that's why Sherry ran to her sister's when things got critical at the Hillcrest. Arty Baxter confirmed my suspicions that Mateo was using the Hillcrest as a front for recruiting women to work at his club and then eventually pressuring them into prostitution. He would cast his net by advertising apartments at the Hillcrest but then only rent to single young vulnerable women. Once they moved into the Hillcrest, he would use a number of different tactics to get them to make the first mistake of going to work at the club for him."

"Tori told me about your suspicions on the ride this morning, but I found it kinda hard to believe," Rico said while shaking his head.

"I know, I know. But knowing Sherry's sister works for the DA's office is just the kind of fortuitous piece of luck I needed to get out from under this mess. As was this letterhead that you snatched for me."

"That's another thing, how's a damn piece of letterhead going to help you?" Rico questioned.

"All in good time big man," Trevor spoke confidently.

"What's up with this 'all in good time' shit?" Rico mimicked Trevor's voice.

"Rico, the master plan is still a work in progress. Give me a break, it's my ass is on the line here," Trevor said in a pleading tone.

Rico rose quickly and spoke authoritatively. "That's another thing Trev; it's your ass on the line because you made it that way. You and Tori could've just moved out of the Hillcrest or called the police when you realized this shit was going down and cut your losses, but you gotta try to play the fuckin knight in shining armor."

"Don't start with that 'Damsel Complex' shit again."

"You know it's true. You haven't changed a bit Trev. It's been a while but it's just like when we were kids. You got a hero complex."

"I told you before I don't agree with you on the damsels thing!" Trevor exclaimed.

A heavy silence fell between them. They stared at each other for a few seconds before Trevor spoke. "Come sit over here and let me fill you in why I wanted the letterhead and how it will hopefully help us to resolve this conflict with Mateo and his crew." He shook his head turned his attention back to the computer.

"But first why don't you take this twenty and go grab us some Reubens at the Floyd's delicatessen down the street. My treat."

"Is that the place that serves those giant-sized sandwiches?"

"Oh yeah."

"Now you're talking Trev. I am hungry as hell."

"Get me a pickles and chips too. Oh, and a Sprite."

"Then you better hit me with another ten spot."

Before Rico walked out the door he turned toward Trevor. "When is the meet?"

"Eight sharp."

"Where are you meeting Mateo at?" Rico said in a low tone.

"Guess?"

"Not that titty club," Rico replied.

"You got it."

"Is that wise? That's his fuckin' turf Trev."

"It's not how I would've planned it but I got no choice. He chose the place, the time, and left no room for negotiations."

"I am coming with!"

"No Rico."

"Trevor don't be stupid brotha! This is some serious shit and I know that the plan that you're about to tell is da bomb plan, but you may need more than just the Duke backing you up dis time."

Trevor stood and slowly walked over to Rico and embraced him. "See, that's what true friendship's really about. You can disagree and argue, but when it comes right down to it? We always have one another's back. Thanks Rico, you're my boy."

"Oh, so you just figured that out? Man, you know it's always been this way and will always be." Rico patted Trevor on the back twice as they hugged.

As they separated, Rico wiped a tear from his eye and tried to change the subject. "Are you going to get an office like this one?"

"Are you kidding me; this is one of Mr. Moncrieff's private offices. I'll be lucky to have a cubical."

Trevor looked at one of the four intricately designed clocks on the wall, each displaying the time in a different time zone around the world. "Damn, it's almost three." He hastily pressed the intercom button on the base of the phone. A warm friendly voice permeated the room. "Yes, Mr. Stillwell, how can I help you?"

"Have you heard anything from Finance on those real estate documents, Ms. Harrisville?" Trevor asked hastily.

"I have them right here, Mr. Stillwell. They were just dropped off. Also Mr. Moncrieff left a message for you. He said to tell you that the finder's commission and cash flow statements look fine. Mr. Rawling from Finance & Acquisitions wants you to double check the title and confirm the check amount before leaving." She hesitated. "Between you and me Mr. Stillwell, he gets a little testy whenever Mr. Moncrieff personally asks him to do something on short notice."

"That's good to know Ms. Harrisville, thanks for the heads up. I'll check the title and other documents in a minute, but can you please read the information on the check to me?"

"Okay, one moment." The intercom transmitted the rustling sound of an envelope opening. "The check is for two hundred and fifty thousand dollars even and made payable to Mr. Arthur H. Baxter. Wait, there's something else in here, it looks like bearer bonds..."

"Don't worry about that, Ms. Harrisville. Thank you very much."

"You're welcome, Mr. Still—"

Trevor quickly interrupted her. "Please call me Trevor."

"Eh…well…okay, I will. Is there anything else?"

"One last thing?" Trevor asked. "Please call Mr. Baxter at the number I gave you earlier and ask him to meet me at First Nation's Bank on Enterprise Avenue in an hour."

"Yes, Mr. Stillwell." With a push of a button the intercom went silent.

"What's that all about Trev?" Rico asked.

"It's all about the plan and if all goes well Mr. Moncrieff will own a piece of property he's wanted for a while and another where he can start developing an entertainment complex project that he's been thinking about."

"What about Mateo? Is he gonna go for this?"

"That's where this letterhead comes in."

"Huh?"

"Rico, don't worry man. I'll explain it all to you while we're eating those sandwiches you were supposed to get ten minutes ago. I can't meet with Mateo on an empty stomach."

"Trevor I can't believe you got jokes at a time like this."

"Rico, serious man. I am starving. I ate a light breakfast early this morning and that's it."

"Au'ight man, I am going right now. But I have one other question."

"Yeah what?"

"Was that woman on the intercom the same one who showed me in?" Trevor nodded in agreement while reviewing the words he typed on the letterhead.

"Damn she's fine. I was trailing behind her as she led me to this office and her ass was just shifting from side to side in that tight black skirt. Damn, she filled that shit out righteously. I don't blame you for flirting with her."

"What? I wasn't flirting with her!" Trevor said with conviction.

"Oh, and I suppose you didn't notice her banging ass, either right?"

"Rico, the Reubens, please man?"

"Okay, I am going!"

"What time is Bruce coming by the Hillcrest to pick you up?" Rico asked as he reached for the doorknob.

"Seven thirty."

"Cool, I'll be there with bells on." Rico closed the door behind him.

Trevor's smile faded as Rico closed the office door behind him. The stark reality of the task at hand weighed on him like a hundred-pound bale of cotton. A strong feeling of dread passed over him like an ocean wave against the shore. He quietly marveled at the absurdity of it all. Despite being faced with uncertainty and danger, his friends were steadfast and resolute. He also knew the events of this evening would be a supreme test of everything he learned in the street and about people. Was he up to the task? Only time would tell. And time was ticking away.

THEY PULLED INTO the unpaved parking lot at precisely 8:00 p.m. The sun was casting its last rays of summer brilliance across the darkening landscape. A familiar figure stood at the entrance of the Secret Palace.

"Who's that?" Rico asked from the backseat.

Bruce quickly answered. "That's Moe, one of Mateo's henchmen that we've been battling for the past two days."

"He looks familiar," Rico muttered.

"You know him?" Trevor replied.

"No, I definitely don't know him but I've seen him some-where before. I just can't put my finger on where."

The car rolled to a stop and all three men exited the car. "Wait here fellas. If I'm not out in twenty minutes, you know what to do." Trevor's eyes moved from Rico to Bruce and were met with a look of reassurance and confidence from both of his friends. Trevor walked in front of the car. Bruce had turned on the headlights and dim light seemed to be trailing behind Trevor as he walked toward the entrance of the club. They highlighted his every step against the creeping shadows of approaching darkness—spotlighting his arrival like an actor toward the stage, and in many ways, Trevor would need a per-formance worthy of an Oscar in order to accomplish his plan.

Trevor slowly approached Moe. "Mateo's waiting inside for you," he said with a scowl. Trevor started for the door when Moe grabbed his arm abruptly. Trevor tensed his body, prepared to throw the first punch. "Relax punk! I just need to pat you down."

It was a thorough pat down and Trevor was glad he didn't take Bruce's advice to strap a piece to his ankle. "I still want a piece of your boy over there," Moe said in a voice that exuded confidence and could barely mask his contempt.

"You sure about that? You know what they say, be careful what you wish for," Trevor responded as he walked away.

As he made his way down the long corridor to the club's inner entrance he thought of the coat-check girl with the long-braided hair and wondered if she was like Tori—an innocent victim—or a willing participant in the lascivious dealings at the club.

Mateo was seated at a table in the center of the club, smoking a cigar and sipping a glass of dark liquid. The smoke from his stogie hung close to his head, obscuring a clear view of his face, only adding to the ominous atmosphere of the half empty club.

Trevor confidently walked over and stood by the table. "Sit the fuck down, what d'you want an engraved invitation or sumthin?" Mateo's words were meant to intimidate but Trevor knew better than to show any hint of fear or hesitation in the presence of his adversary. He slowly pulled a chair out a clear foot or so away from the table and sat, crossing his legs, showing Mateo that he was completely relaxed and not at all intimidated.

Mateo stared intently at him, taking a visual measure of the man seated across from him. "So you wanted to talk to me about sumthin." Mateo spoke in that same husky voice that Trevor first heard when he accosted the women outside his Hillcrest apartment window.

Trevor made a mental note not to return the same hostile tone when he spoke. He knew that if his tone was interpreted as threatening it would be met with an equally hostile and combative response. If his plan were to work, he would have to get Mateo to acquiesce to it—coercion or intimidation would not work with Mateo.

"I've come across a letter I think you may want to see." Trevor slowly and deliberately reached into his pocket and slid the envelope with the letter inside across the table toward Mateo.

Mateo didn't acknowledge it at first. He placed his elbows on the table and rested his chin on his clasped hands. He looked Trevor squarely in the eyes for a few seconds before reaching down and opening the envelope.

As he read it, his face slightly contorted and Trevor thought he sensed a slight diminishment in Mateo's bravado—a chink in his armor. Trevor smiled to himself.

"How'd you get this?" Mateo asked in a slightly agitated tone.

"A friend," Trevor responded very calmly in a very relaxed voice.

"A friend, huh? Figures. It's always a mutherfuckin' friend wit guys like you." Mateo smiled slyly. "So why'd dis so-called friend of yours gives this letter to you in the first place?"

"Because I paid him for it," Trevor said in a calm but stern tone.

"That still don't answer the why."

"I knew that it was a valuable piece of information and information is power. I am always interested in acquiring information that may serve my interest," Trevor replied, trying to stay relaxed and reduce the level of anxiety slowly building within.

"So what the fuck do you want?" Mateo demanded with a wicked scowl across his face, which sent a chill through Trevor's body.

"It's not what I want; it's what you want," Trevor responded.

"Huh? What's dis letter gotta do with you?"

"It's simple. I paid for the letter because I though it presented an opportunity that could be mutually beneficial."

"What's in it for you?"

"The Hillcrest."

"What the fuck's my Hillcrest gotta do with dis?"

"I represent a man who's interested in obtaining Hillcrest but I know Mr. Baxter, who owns it on paper, doesn't have any control over it because of a debt he owes to you."

"Like I said, my mutherfuckin' Hillcrest."

Trevor didn't reply. He just stared at Mateo.

"Go 'head. This is gettin' interesting." Mateo took another long draw from his cigar.

"Here's the deal: A few weeks ago, the DA's office caught wind of your little business operations at the Fox Trot. The DA assigned this friend of mine to do the initial investigation and make a recommendation. That letter represents what he found, which says there's enough evidence to mount a formal investigation and maybe to get an indictment against you." Trevor took another envelope out of his pocket. "But here is another letter, which says that my friend found no evidence to support an investigation of you or your business dealings. Which letter the DA sees depends on what happens right now between you and me."

"Let me get dis straight, if we can work somethin' out then the DA never even starts their investigation on me."

"Yes, it is really that simple. This second letter states that there's no grounds for any investigation."

Mateo picked up the second letter and looked it over.

"You must be a pretty influential nigga 'round here to have dat much influence over things." Trevor didn't reply, knowing that Mateo was trying to bait him.

"So, what's the deal?" Mateo continued.

"It's simple. I pay off Mr. Baxter's debt to you and you move your operations back to Edgewood or elsewhere, but not here, and the DA gets this second letter."

"Sumthin' not right. Why do you or your friend at the DA

care about Arty's debt to me?" Mateo narrowed his stare, locking in on Trevor.

"My friend at the DA doesn't really give a damn? My friend's getting paid for playing his role but come Monday morning a letter gets put on the DA's desk. It's your choice which one gets put there." Trevor showed no signs of the growing sense of apprehension in his gut.

Trevor continued, "The only thing the DA sees on Monday morning is a letter from his lead investigator saying that there is no evidence to support any allegations against you and the case is closed."

"Okay, so what you got for me?" Mateo seemed intrigued.

"Mr. Baxter owes you twenty grand, right?" Trevor said assuredly.

"That's right; he owes me twenty large plus interest."

"Interest? It seems to me that you've been earning interest on that original twenty through this club," Trevor said as he looked around. Mateo was forcing him into a more aggressive stand than he wanted to take.

"That might be true if dis place was making me some real money, but bidniz has been slow, you know what I mean." Mateo leaned forward and touched the center of the table for no apparent reason. Trevor found Mateo's mannerisms as strange as his voice was grating.

Trevor acted like he was considering his next move when in fact he had scripted this scene in his mind over and over again. "Thirty grand, that's the final offer, take it or leave it."

"Cash."

"No, bearer bonds. With no interest coupon payments but three bonds with ten thousand dollars face value each." Trevor wanted to smile but held it back. He learned from Arty that Mateo was enamored with bearer bonds since watching some TV shows on the benefit of bearer bonds.

"Dat works." Mateo smiled.

Trevor knew that he would love the bond aspect of his offer and for the first time he noticed that Mateo smiled a normal, non-menacing smile.

Mateo's smile quickly disappeared. "Not that it is any of your fucking business but I hate dis fuckin' town. I cain't run my girls on the street because of these righteous ass cops and dis club is a fucking money pit. You see Kim, unlike you, I don't like working." Mateo's use of Trevor's Christian name caused a knot to form in his stomach.

"Working a nine-to-five is for suckers. Pimpin' bitches is really no work to me. Shit, they do all the work. I get all the money and free pussy too. What more could a nigga ask for." Trevor could feel his disgust for Mateo swelling inside his chest, but kept his face devoid of emotion as he listened.

"Easy money that's what I'm about." Mateo took a quick sip from his glass. "So, taking your thirty large and shutting down this little operation seems like easy money to me." *It can't be this easy,* Trevor thought to himself. *Could there actually be a light at the end of this tunnel?*

"But I don't like feelin' that I'm being run to of town. First you infiltrate my pussy castle at the Hillcrest, then you fuck up my boy Roscoe, and now you're trying to bushwhack me and kick me out of town. I can't have that. I do have a reputation to keep up." Mateo gripped the corner of the table as he spoke.

Trevor felt an instant and overwhelming sense of foreboding. He knew his bluff was in jeopardy of being called. He reacted instinctively.

Deviating from his well-thought-out script, Trevor quickly responded, "No one else knows about this but you and I. Mr. Baxter thinks I'm making you a business offer for your interest in the Hillcrest. He doesn't know anything about the letter. No one knows about the letter other than you, me, and the investigator at the DA's office.

"So, you can call it whatever you want to, it really doesn't matter to me. You really don't lose any face, plus look where you're at if you refuse. You're out an easy $30K and you still have the DA to deal with. An astute businessman such as yourself can clearly see that this offer is a win-win for you." Trevor hated pandering to Mateo's ego but this was no time for such pettiness. He was pulling out all the stops.

Mateo twirled the small scotch glass in his hand. Trevor thought to himself, *He's not going for it, what will I do next?*

He decided to make a final move and if Mateo didn't act then it was over, and all hell was going to break loose. "Okay, if that's the way you want it." Trevor reached to retrieve the letter.

"Hold up man. I didn't say nothing yet." Mateo leaned back in his chair and looked Trevor squarely in the eye—looking, probing for a sign of weakness. "I got sort of a counter offer of sorts for ya."

"Go on." Trevor returned Mateo's deadpan stare.

"There's only one thing that I like more than fine pussy and that's gambling," Mateo said, full of uncompromising hubris.

"And your point is?" Trevor was growing tired of the sound of Mateo's raspy voice.

"A wager," Mateo said sinisterly.

"What kind of wager?"

"The only kind there is, one where there's a winner and a loser!" Mateo smiled insidiously.

"Can you be more specific?" Trevor felt as though he was about to lose control.

"It's like this: If you win, I'll take the money and go. If you lose, I'll still take the money and I'll stay here in town. Oh, and the DA still gets that second letter either way." Mateo cracked a crooked smile.

"Sounds like you win either way."

"Son, that's the only way I do things," Mateo said as he rose from the table.

"BRUCE YOU DON'T have to do this! I'll figure another way out of this," Trevor frantically pleaded with his friend.

"Trev, you know me man. You know this is the best way to end this whole thing. Besides, when have I ever turned down a challenge to knuckle up? I been wantin' a piece of that Moe since day one. I was dreaming about this fine little piece of ass that I usta rock back in high school when they bushwhacked us. He ruined a perfect good dream. He's gotta pay for that."

Trevor knew that Bruce was only kidding and that his use of levity was a veiled attempt to mask his building fury.

Mateo and Moe were waiting under the spotlight at the rear of the lot. The three of them approached without saying a word. Rico was visibly nervous, but his husky frame cast an imposing figure nonetheless.

"Mateo, this doesn't have to go down like this," Trevor barked.

"Hey, I'm a gambling man, what can I say?" Mateo smiled and leaned against a fence that surrounded the parking lot.

"Damn man, your voice is grating and getting on my last nerve. Can you just shut up!" Bruce's words were laced with an intensity that was palpable.

"Relax tough guy, your battle's wit' my protégé here, Maurice 'Bloodstone' Braxton. You may remember him as the former middleweight Golden Gloves Champion. He is my ace boon-coon and the man who's going to whup your ass."

"I knew I remembered him from somewhere," Rico mumbled to himself as a look of concern traversed his face. He was a huge boxing fan and had not missed a championship fight in many years. He collected all the boxing magazines and could name the last five champions in almost every weight division. Rico definitely fancied himself a boxing aficionado. He was visibly upset with himself for not recognizing Moe sooner.

Trevor's throat constricted then went dry with the realization that Moe was really the dangerous one. He thought the sheer size and bulk of Roscoe made him the main physical threat, forgetting that size meant nothing when it came to toughness and fighting ability. Something clearly epitomized by his five-foot-nine friend standing beside him.

Maurice removed his shirt and displayed the upper body of a toned, ripped, well-conditioned boxer. He was lean and wiry, with a stomach as toned and muscular as any Trevor had ever seen on the cover of fitness magazines. Trevor looked at Bruce, and if Bruce was impressed with the physical condition of his opponent, his expressionless face didn't show it.

Bruce took off his shirt and displayed a stomach lined with row after row of protruding muscles. His arms and chests looked like a thin layer of skin was stretched tightly over muscles of stone.

Both men began to stretch and loosen up. Bruce dropped to the ground and quickly pumped out ten one-handed push-ups. After a few jumping jacks and a hamstring stretch, he declared himself ready by a stern nod to Trevor. Maurice finished his stretching routine, which included some lightning quick shadow boxing and ended with a few deep knee bends.

Mateo spoke into a small megaphone. "Here are da rules, and there aren't many. But we are gonna do dis how they do it on the West Coast. I'll keep the time and there will be two minutes of action, two minutes of rest. You fight until one man can no longer stand or just quits. No foreign objects so you cain't pick up anything and use it as a weapon.

"You got that Kim." Mateo looked at Trevor and smiled. Mateo was positioned directly under the parking light and was basking in the roles of fight promoter, announcer, and trainer.

Trevor didn't say a word, nor did he acknowledge Mateo's question, he knew that Mateo was trying to get under his skin by calling him Kim. Trevor paid no attention; he just placed his hand on Bruce's shoulder and whispered something.

Bruce listened intently. "Gotcha," was all that Bruce said in response to what Trevor had whispered to him.

"Ready! Time in!" Mateo barked into the megaphone. "FIGHT!!!"

Bruce slowly approached Moe with his hands held high. His left fist was level with his chest while his right hand was close to his head. The two combatants began circling each other.

Moe struck the first blow, landing a solid left jab to Bruce's head just above his right eyebrow. That opened up a three-inch gash. Blood poured into Bruce's eye.

"Youra bleeder huh?" Moe said as he peppered Bruce with several more jabs followed by a vicious left hook that just missed Bruce's head. For the next minute no blows were thrown. Both men just circled one another, sizing each other up.

"Time out!"

Bruce walked over to Trevor and Rico. "Trev, this nigga can toss his hands and he is fast as hell but watch me take his ass out."

Trevor wiped the blood off Bruce's face with a white towel he had retrieved from Bruce's car. Bruce was fanatical about cleaning his car so there was always a set of brand new short white towels in his trunk. Then he used it to apply pressure to the cut itself.

"Here, drink some of this." Trevor handed Bruce an open bottle of apple juice Rico had brought with him.

"Apple juice?" Bruce looked curiously at Trevor. "Trevor, as a corner man you leave a lot to be desired."

"I wasn't ready to be a corner man tonight."

"I know, but lucky for you I am always ready to toss my fists."

"Ready. Time in! FIGHT!!!"

Moe picked up the pace of the fight by throwing a multitude of lightning quick punches which overwhelmed Bruce's defenses. He was struck hard by a few solid jabs to the head. And again, the blood flowed. Moe was fast, much faster than Bruce. In fact, he was faster than anyone Trevor had ever seen in person. Each jab connected with a solid thud on Bruce's head and face. Bruce tried to step to the side of Moe's lethal left jab but ended up right in the line of fire for Moe's power punch: a right hook. The hook landed right below Bruce's left ear.

"Time out!"

Bruce walked toward Trevor and Rico with a dazed look in his eyes. Trevor whispered to Bruce, "Forget about waiting, you should do it now."

Bruce, whose face was battered, spoke between deep and hurried breaths. "No Trev, not yet. I gotta wait otherwise it won't work. Trust me on this one."

The megaphone cracked to life "Time in. Ready, FIGHT!!!"

Bruce smartly decided to close the distance between him and Moe and step inside of Moe's punches, but he knew that he would have to take some major punishment to get there. They stood toe-to-toe, neither of them yielding an inch as they traded punch after punch, an awesome display of boxing skill by Moe and pure toughness by Bruce. Trevor wanted to turn away but his body wouldn't respond—he was transfixed. Trevor noticed out of the corner of his eye Rico wincing with every punch that Bruce was hit with. In his mind he was fighting alongside Bruce.

A straight right rocked Bruce. Instinctively Bruce raised his guard much high than usual to protect his face; that opened up his ribs and stomach. Moe attacked Bruce's body with a series of punches before going back upstairs and badly hurting him with a solid right cross. Bruce tried to move away. Moe gave chase and landed several short but powerful punches. By the time Mateo called an end to that two-minute period it was quite obvious to everyone watching that Moe was in complete control of the fight. His confidence was soaring while Bruce's face looked like he'd been in a car accident. His face was swelling at a fast rate.

A small crowd gathered and a few of the men there started betting on the fight. Not surprisingly all the early money was on Moe.

"Ready. FIGHT!" Mateo smiled broadly and it was obvious that he was really enjoying Moe's dominant performance. His confidence was soaring.

For the next two minutes there was not a whole lot of action. Moe stalked Bruce around the cordoned off area and inflicted damage whenever he found an opening. Bruce was on the defense; he tried to attack Moe but couldn't corner him or nail him with one of the several roundhouse rights he threw.

Then seemingly out of nowhere, Bruce landed a hard-right hand and a left hook that seemed to momentarily stun his opponent. Moe backed up and Bruce landed a straight left and right hook, but Moe's balance and footwork were flawless so he quickly moved out of range. Bruce tried to follow a with straight right hand right down the pike but Moe quickly countered with a hard over-head right. Bruce was stunned. Moe regrouped and unleashed a furry of ten consecutive punches. Bruce stumbled backward as more blood streaked down his face.

Moe was every bit the boxer that Mateo had boasted, he possessed a lethal combination of speed, finesse and power, but instead of pressing his assault he stopped momentarily it seemed to admire his handiwork. "You're not so bad when you don't have a baseball bat, huh, tough guy?" Moe asked as he stood waiting for Bruce to step forward again.

Bruce, undaunted and unimpressed by bravado, seized the opportunity that Moe had created by stopping to taunt him. He stepped toward Moe and feigned a jab; Moe quickly threw up his defense and leaned away from the direction of the fake. Bruce quickly threw a short right hook that caught Moe flush on the top of the head. The force of the blow incapacitated him momentarily and his legs quivered, but Bruce was off balance after throwing that hook and couldn't capitalize on that advantage. For the next twenty seconds, Moe got the best of Bruce by jabbing his lightning quick left into Bruce's face and moving away whenever Bruce got close enough to counterpunch.

"Time out."

"Let me see your right hand," Trevor said to Bruce once he had walked over to where Trevor and Rico were standing. He reluctantly lifted his right hand. His right hand looked deformed and two of his knuckles were not where they should be.

"Damn, Duke. Let's call this fight," Trevor pleaded.

"You can't continue to fight with only your left hand," Rico added.

"Just watch me," Bruce said with steely determination.

"Time in. Ready FIGHT!"

Bruce threw a wild left that Moe easily avoided. Then Moe took the offensive. He saw an opening and landed a hard-right hook to Bruce's forehead. It was the hardest punch either had landed. Bruce took several steps backward and was in retreat for most of the remaining time.

"Time out."

The timbre of Mateo voice echoed his confidence, and he had a perpetual smile etched on his face.

As Bruce wiped the sweat and blood off his face, Trevor thought that this battle between these two men of steel constitutions, one an irresistible force, the other an immovable object, could result in a death. That thought had never entered his mind before, but seeing his friend bleed out the way he was, it worried him. He knew that Moe was emboldened by the busted up face of his opponent. But Trevor did notice that Bruce had indeed inflicted damage of his own over the course of the fight. Moe's legs and balance were slightly compromised. It wasn't as visual as the crimson blanket that covered Bruce, but to Trevor it was the sign he was looking for.

Trevor whispered in Bruce's ear again, but this time Bruce nodded in agreement. "Make this a street fight now! Drag it into the gutter. You waited long enough. He has completely forgotten that this is a street fight. You boxed him for so long that his boxing instincts have taken over. Once you flip the script on him, he won't be able to adjust in time. But Bruce you got to take him out quick, fast and in a hurry."

"Time in! Ready, FIGHT!!!"

Moe feigned a left and threw a forceful right uppercut that caught Bruce on the chin; he dropped him to a knee. Moe quickly closed in to inflict more damage. That was just what Bruce was hoping for. Acting more hurt than he actually was, was a ploy that worked to lure Moe in closer. Bruce sprung upward, tackling him by the waist. But this wasn't accomplished without incurring some major punishment. As he leapt, Maurice got off a series of punches to the back of Bruce's head and neck that again caused Trevor to cringe.

Once on the ground his grappling and street fighting skills took the forefront as Bruce established control of the fight. What really made Bruce an outstanding street fighter is that he studied a multitude of fighting disciples. He was an MMA fighter before anyone knew what mixed martial arts was. He started studying judo when he was thirteen and Muay Thai a year later.

Bruce quickly maneuvered into position and captured Moe's head in a vise-like headlock. For the next few seconds, Bruce applied pressure to Moe's neck while pounding his powerful left hand into Moe's face and head, but without much leverage. His punches were much less destructive but served their purpose. Moe countered by planting several firm elbows into Bruce's stomach.

Suddenly Bruce did something that those who witnessed it would never forget. He quickly released the headlock, rolled over onto Maurice's back and slid down to the back of Moe's legs just below his knees. Moe, thinking he was free, tried to get up by doing a push-up-like motion. Bruce used Moe's upward momentum to his advantage. He secured Moe's ankles under his armpits, quickly ascended to a standing position lifting Moe's legs, waist then torso off the ground. Once standing Bruce started swinging Moe around in a 360-degree spin. After three strong rotations, Bruce released his grip on Moe, sending him careening into the front grille of Mateo's Bentley some fifteen feet away. His body crumpled like a discarded mannequin against the unforgiving steel of the car. Unbelievably, Moe tried valiantly to regain his feet, but his body betrayed him and he sagged into a heap on the dirt. The epic battle was over. The small crowd applauded the victor.

Bruce took a few steps toward Trevor and Rico before dropping to one knee again. Trevor, who had been keeping one eye on the fight and the other on Mateo, grabbed Bruce's arm, assisting him to his feet. He then slowly approached his nemesis still standing under the spotlight.

"I guess that's that," Mateo said as Trevor cautiously but deliberately approached him.

"I guess so, but I don't see what was gained by this little display," Trevor replied as he handed Mateo a large manila envelope with the bearer bonds. Trevor kept his right hand free. He was ready to quickly extract the pistol hidden at the small of his back at the slightest provocation. During the fight, Rico managed to slip a gun to Trevor without being detected by Mateo or anyone else.

"Man, I am a true hustler. I am a pimp and a player. That just how I roll," Mateo said he turned away and walked toward his car. "Tell your boy if ever wants ta make some real money ta look me up in Edgewood. I got some connections that could put some large dollars in his pockets. And it seems that I have some unexpected cash to invest in some new talent." Mateo shook the envelope over his head with his free hand.

"Yeah sure, I'll do that," Trevor responded.

"Oh, and tell that little honey of yours I said to stay sweet." Mateo laughed as he opened the door to his Bentley. His words enraged Trevor; he wanted to rush over and tackle him. Instead he clenched his fist until it started to throb. Then he exhaled and released his fist and with it all the tension and anxiety melted away.

Trevor watched as dirt sprung up and formed a small dust cloud behind Mateo's spinning rear tires. Trevor walked over to Bruce who was lying down and resting comfortable along the backseat of his car. "Is everything cool, Trev?" he said as he coughed up blood.

"Yeah Duke, everything's cool, but let's get you to a hospital."

"**STOP IT TREVOR!** Please…STOP IT!" Her pleas did not slow his aggressive actions. "Trevor! I'm serious, please stop!" He continued to tickle her stomach and thighs as she tried to make a hasty escape, rolling toward the foot of the bed. "Please Trevor, come on now stop…you know how ticklish I am!" Tori's laughter filled the four corners of the room each time his nimble fingers found their mark.

"Trevor, we have so much to do and we're not even close to unpacking all my stuff yet, so stop tickling me or we'll never finish." She jumped off the bed and straightened her blouse.

"Come on Trevor, get serious please, I want to get this done today so we can spend all day tomorrow relaxing. You know it's supposed to rain all day and you know what that means." Tori said with a seductive tone.

Trevor stretched out on the bed, locking his fingers behind his head and crossing his legs at the ankle. "Spending an entire rainy day relaxing with you, watching movies, eating Chinese and making love, uh, let me think about it."

"Trevor seriously," she replied with a smile. "Not that I don't like my new apartment but I don't see why we don't move in together."

Trevor didn't mention The Apartment Daydream of his youth to anyone—not Bruce, not Rico, not even his mother knew about that childhood daydream that occupied so much of his thoughts back then.

So how could he explain to Tori why he couldn't live with her? He couldn't so he did the next best thing, he changed topic.

"Tori, I am going to see if Rico has settled in."

"Okay Trevor, I get it, but this conversation isn't over yet."

Trevor jumped up out of the bed and started to walk out of the bedroom. "Oh, and tell Rico I said hello too?"

"No problem, baby girl," was Trevor's reply.

THE FIRST THING he did was change the nameplate on the door. It now read: Rico A. Cubberson, Apartment Manager. When Trevor offered him the job, it was the first thing that he wanted to do. See his name on that nameplate.

The door was slightly ajar when Trevor arrived. He nudged it open and stood silently in the archway. Cardboard boxes were piled everywhere. A series of mismatched furniture and odd accessories cluttered every inch of the living room. There was a fuzzy orange beanbag chair and a black ashtray in the shape of an outstretched hand.

He stood there silently, watching Rico carefully moving around the clutter while singing to music that was playing in the background. It became clear after only a few moments that he was locked in a futile attempt to arrange the mess that lay before him. As quickly as he cleared one area, he would place another item in its place.

"Damn Rico do you have enough stuff or what?" Trevor announced his presence.

Rico skillfully maneuvered around several packing boxes of virtually every size and shape to greet his friend with a hand-shake and a hug. "C'mon Trev, you had to know that my mom would overdo it. She's trying to give me everything she's saved for the past forty years. I think she's using me movin' out as an excuse for cleaning out the garage, the basement, and the attic."

"Sure looks that way," was Trevor's response. Despite the disarray surrounding him, Trevor could clearly see that he was excited to have this opportunity. Trevor's best friend in the world was happy and that made Trevor feel good.

"Damn Rico, that coffee table looks like something out of an old *Shaft* flick, man. How old is it?" he asked rhetorically. "Should go well with your Vanity 6 poster. And what's the deal with that table?" It was a purple oval-shaped coffee table with three separate tiers.

Rico barked out a quick, short laugh.

Trevor continued scanning the room. "And that beanbag chair, damn Rico, it's green and what is that, suede?! You won't ever catch me in that, ever."

"You can crack all the jokes you like and nothin' gonna change the fact that you're THE MUTHERFUCKIN MAN!!" Rico said emphatically.

"Hey man, you told me you needed a new job, right?"

"Right," Rico replied.

"And you said you needed your own place because you were tired of living with your mom, right?"

"Right again."

"And I told you that as soon as things cleared up for me, I would help you out because you're my boy, right?"

"Like a' said Trev, you da man. You not only hooked a brotha up with a sweet gig as the super of this joint but I get this funky basement crib on the bubble too. Arty is crazy for letting this shit go."

"Hey man, I'm just glad it all worked out. When Mr. Moncrieff decided to buy the Hillcrest, I knew he would be looking for a new apartment manager so I told him I knew a reliable carpenter handyman type brother who was looking for free rent…" Trevor started laughing before he could finish the sentence.

"Get the hell outta here Trev, you didn't say that, did you?" Rico replied.

"Well, I left out the stuff about you needing free rent. But listen, there's one other condition to the job that I forgot to tell you about," he said, tone changing to a more serious one.

"What's that?" Rico asked, showing a deep look of concern.

"You have to change your name to Mr. Bookman." Trevor started to sing the theme to the TV sitcom *Good Times*. "Good Times, keeping your head above water, making a wave when you can. A temporary layoff, good times…Ain't we lucky we got them…Gooood Tiiiimes."

Rico's reaction went from concern to relief to uncontrolled laughter. "You a trip man. Always got jokes. But I ain't mad at ya 'cause with this hookup you can call me Booger Bookman if you want. I'll even start wearing farmer jeans too."

"Damn Rico, there you go again taking all the fun out of my jokes by going along with it."

"Hey, what can I say Trev?" he replied as he walked into the kitchen. "Do you want something to drink?"

"No, I'm cool. I just came down to see how you were making out. I got to get upstairs, I got some work to do."

"Work, work?" Rico asked.

"Yeah, I am working on a special project for Mr. Moncrieff."

Rico returned from the kitchen with a diet Coke in hand but he seemed lost in his thoughts. "I still can't believe you duped Mateo that easily."

"Who said it was easy?" Trevor wasn't disillusioned and wasn't about to make light of the situation. He knew that some truly fortuitous events had come into play. He knew that they all were very lucky to make it out of that situation unscathed, never mind coming out on top. God was watching over them during this whole fiasco.

"Trevor, let me ask you this hypothetical: What happens if Mateo decides to check with your someone in the DA's office and finds out that the letter, the investigation...that all that shit was bogus?" Rico asked between gulps of soda.

"If he does, we'll do what we've been doing our whole lives: we'll deal with it," Trevor said firmly. "But it's not likely. I found out through Arty that Mateo is terrified of the DA. Something about his dad getting put away by a DA. I don't think he wants anything to do with contacting the DA, especially since he thinks he's in the clear."

Trevor spoke confidently but the question caused his thoughts to drift to a dark place. What if Mateo return? What would Trevor have to do to protect himself and the ones he loved?

Rico recognized that Trevor's thoughts were going to a dark place so he decided to reassure his friend and try to change the topic. "I think you're right Trev, that shit's over and done with. For sure.

"Trev, did I tell you that my mom's been here twice already today with fat plates of food for breakfast and lunch? I tried to tell her that I'm on a diet, trying to lose weight, but she won't listen. I think she gonna drive me crazy, man.

"Oh yeah Trev, I almost forgot...she dropped this by earlier too." Rico reached into his back pocket. "It's a letter from Bruce addressed to you. He sent it to my mom's house. I guess he decided to play it safe and mail it to a place he knew wasn't going to change anytime soon. My mom's been living there for the past forty years and she'll been there for the next forty, God willing."

Trevor took the letter from Rico. "I am going up to my place. Check you out later."

"Alright Trev," Rico said in a concerned tone.

"Yeah man. I guess it's just all starting to hit me."

"It's over Trev. And we're still standing. It's all good."

"True, true. I'll get back at you."

As Trevor ascended the staircase heading to his apartment on the third floor, he could feel the weight of the past week building on his shoulders with every step he took.

With one big shrug of his shoulder and twist of his neck, the weight dissipated. He entered his apartment. Tori had left a note telling him that she went to her place to finish unpacking.

Trevor slowly opened the letter and began reading.

Trev,

You are my ace boon coon, man. I don't know how to thank you for the five large you gave me. I know that in your mind I deserved it for tangling with Moe, but you know that I'll knuckle up for free. And Rico let it slip that the $5,000 was your finder's fee for hooking your boss up on the Hill-crest. Regardless thanks man. That little honey of yours is very cool. Try to make that work. Can see why she had you all twisted. Just messing with you, Trev. Who knows, maybe I'LL get a marriage invitation and then be baby Trevor's godfather? Just fuckin' with you Trev.

Cally is cool. The first day here my cousin Abner got me a little part-time job working in a junkyard. And like I promised you no criminal shit. I'll be sleeping on Ab's couch until I can find a cheap crib. I think I will like it out here. No one knows me so it should be easier staying out of trouble. I'm gonna find me a nice honey and settle down, like you. I can't say that I will call soon because you know how much I hate talking on the phone but I will drop you a note every once in a while. Of course, you can look me up if you're out this way anytime any day. And I'll do the same if I get back there for a visit.

Peace and much love—Bruce Eric Peterson III

BRUCE HAD ONLY been in California for only a few days, but Trevor couldn't help worrying about him. Trevor was concerned about Bruce's probation status. They both knew that if he was found to be in another state then his probation would be violated. The letter went a long way toward easing his concern. Someone knocked at the door. "Come in."

"Trev, I forgot to tell you how those tenant meetings went last night." Rico walked in.

"Damn, how did I forget to ask you about that? I have a 8:00 a.m. meeting with Mr. Moncrieff tomorrow. I got to get my shit together quick, fast and in a hurry." Trevor shook his head as he spoke.

"Trev, don't be so hard on yourself, man. You've been under a lot of pressure. You'll get it together; I got faith in my brother."

"Thanks Rico." Trevor continued, "So give me the skinny on the tenant meetings?"

"I met with most of them last night as a group and I have individual meetings for those who couldn't make it."

"Do you need some help with them?" Trevor inquired.

"Who? The girls, or the meeting?" A sly smile crept across Rico's face.

"I'm being serious, Rico."

"Nah, I got it. I'm doing exactly what we talked about. For the women we know who were pressured into working at the club, I offered them three months' free rent until they could get back on their feet. I told them about the new management and policies. And for those needing help finding new jobs, I hooked them up with the employment job bank at that community development agency Mr. Moncrieff recommended."

Rico continued, "And speaking of Mr. Moncrieff, he is cool as shit too. His company hired several of the girls and several others he gave internships and even partial scholarships to the community college."

Rico looked and took a deep breath, signaling to Trevor that a more troubling matter was next. "From what I've learned, Mateo had put pressure on more than half the women in the Crest to start working at the club. Some weren't down and were in the process of trying to move out. Others decided to work there. Some had just started, others had been working there a month or so. After working at the club for a month or so Mateo would start turning the screws on the women, trying to convince them that they could get rich; first by dancing at the club then by selling ass."

He continued. "It's funny, Mateo had yet to approach the majority of the women living at the Crest, but according to your boy Arty, Mateo was going to hit them all up over the next few months. Believe it or not, a few even decided to go to Chicago with him. Guess not everyone wanted to be rescued, huh?" Rico asked, puzzled.

"Hey Rico, I am not passing judgment on the women who decided to go with Mateo. Pimps have a certain power over certain women; it has always been that way. Rico, you know that as well as I do," Trevor replied.

"Yeah, I guess you're right, Trev. Anyway, the way I see it there will probably be six to twelve vacancies when it's all said and done." Rico finished off the can of diet soda with a huge gulp.

"Well, Mr. Big-Time Apartment Manager, I think you should get that ad ready for this Sunday's paper and line up the cleaning crew to have those apartments ready to go for next month. Mr. Moncrieff's a nice guy but don't let that fool you; he's an astute businessman, first and foremost. He's invested some serious cash into this place and he expects it to be fully occupied and making him some money soon. You know what I mean."

"Trev, don't worry man. I'm on it like Blue Bonnet. I got this job down, paperwork and everything. This place be runnin' as smoothly as the engine on a BMW, you'll see."

"I'm proud of you, man."

Trevor continued. "You know despite the fact that some of the girls decided to continue that lifestyle, the ones that we helped will look at you as their savior."

"Maybe so Trev, but we know you're the real hero here, brotha."

"We all played our part Rico, but the women here at the Crest are gonna know you as being the man that saved the day. Can you handle that?"

"SSSShit, damn right I can!" Rico quickly replied.

"Maybe, but what happens when they start fawning all over you? You know: throwing themselves at you. Asking if you need a backrub, inviting you over for a late-night dinners. That could be trouble. You are an employee of the Hillcrest Apartments LLC."

"Trev, you know you're not the only ladies' man in this world. I can hold my own with the honeys, but business is business and business and pleasure don't mix."

"I hear what you are saying and trust your judgment, Rico. I really do, man," Trevor said.

"Trev, so what did Bruce have to say?" Trevor looked at the letter. He had momentarily forgotten that it was in his hand.

"Nothing major. He just wanted to let me know he was okay," Trevor replied.

"If it wasn't for him, shit could've gone south, huh?"

"You ain't said nothing, Rico. I really don't know where things would have ended up if not for Bruce. He pulled my fat out of the fire twice over the past week."

After a few moments of silent contemplation by both of them, Rico verbalized what they both were thinking. "Do you think he'll be au'right in Cally?"

Trevor stood motionless as he let Rico's words sink in. Resonating deep within him and generating a flow of emotions and concerns.

"Trev, you au'ight man. You spacin' out on me or somtin'?"

"Rico, I am cool...just thinking about what you said." Trevor sighed deeply. "Things are much different in Cally, there's a lot of trouble he could get into out there."

"You worried?" asked Rico.

"Bruce is the Duke, as unchanging as the tide, so, no, I am really not worried...but I do know one thing for certain: that if he ever needs me, I'll be there in a heartbeat."

"We both will, Trev, we both will," Rico said as he walked out the door.

Trevor walked over to the black leather couch and collapsed into its soft inviting comfort. He looked around the room and realized that this was the first time since the day he first walked into this apartment that he could just relax and appreciate his accomplishments. Everything around the girls at the Hillcrest, Tori, Moe and Roscoe, Sherry and Mateo all happened in the first week of him moving into his dream apartment. The week was so hectic and tense that he had also forgotten that he made that childhood daydream a reality. As he continued to look around the room, he nodded and thought to himself, this was even better than the daydream. Trevor knew that seldom does reality match the fantasy. But as he looked around his spacious apartment he knew that at least in his case the reality surpassed the fantasy of his childhood daydream.

Trevor closed his eyes; he couldn't help but think what the future held considering what the first week in his new apartment had been like. He hoped that the events of the last week were an aberration; that his life would settle down into a more mundane existence, but somehow knew that wouldn't be the case for Kimbro Trevor Stillwell.

FIN

Made in the USA
Middletown, DE
02 August 2021